Bryn Mathieson just had to be the most infuriating man she had ever met, Tara decided angrily—bossing her about and doing his best to ruin her peaceful Pacific island holiday. But, as the island suddenly turned from Paradise into a nightmare, she found she couldn't do without him—in more ways than one . . .

SAVAGE SUMMER

BY

SUE PETERS

MILLS & BOON LIMITED
15–16 BROOK'S MEWS
LONDON W1A 1DR

First published 1984
Australian copyright 1984
Philippine copyright 1984
This edition 1984

© Sue Peters 1984

ISBN 0 263 74624 0

Set in Monophoto Plantin 10 on 11 pt.
01–0584 – 45489

Made and printed in Great Britain by
Richard Clay (The Chaucer Press) Ltd,
Bungay, Suffolk

CHAPTER ONE

'ARE you crazy, parking under coconut palms in a gale like this?'

He was fair, so he wasn't a local. And he did not look like a hippie. He was clean, as well as clean-shaven. His open-necked shirt and shorts were their original white, and his light brown hair, bleached lighter still at the front by exposure to the sun, was neatly cut close to his finely shaped head. But if he wasn't a local, or a hippie, who was he? His torso, or as much of it as was not covered by his brief shirt and shorts, was burned mahogany, arguing a life in the open air, but there was a purposefulness about the cut of his features, about his stride, that told Tara he was someone to be reckoned with. Tensely, she watched him approach across the sand, and all the warnings she chose to ignore when she set out on her tour rose in a frightening rush to confront her.

'Don't travel alone, you're asking for trouble. At least if you do, take a dog along with you, or something to protect yourself with.'

'Cancel the holiday, Tara.' Peggy had telephoned from Vancouver, and added her quota to the good advice. 'We'll arrange another holiday together later, as soon as my broken ankle's mended.'

'I'll be quite safe in the caravanette.' Tara laughed her friend's fears to scorn. 'I'm quite capable of taking care of myself.'

'There are hippies on the Pacific islands, the same as there are everywhere else,' Peggy persisted worriedly. 'For all their talk of universal love, their feelings may not be purely platonic, to a girl travelling on her own.

5

Especially to an attractive one. Take the caravanette back to the hire company,' she urged, 'and explain about my accident. They'll refund the hire fee and we can take it out again together later in the year when my leg's out of plaster, and I'm mobile again. You could stay in Hawaii for a couple of weeks,' she suggested. 'Be lazy for a change, like any other tourist.'

'I'll think about it,' Tara promised blithely, and did no more than that. Hawaii did not attract her. As a seasoned courier for a holiday travel firm, she saw enough of the tourist resorts during her working life. For her own holidays, she preferred to go off the beaten track, and a caravanette was the ideal transport to enable her to be completely free, and independent. As for taking a dog along, the thought alarmed her far more than the remote possibility of being set upon and robbed during her travels.

'There aren't any hippies on Mahila,' she argued. 'A sugar company set up a plantation there, but even they pulled out because the small size made the operation uneconomic. From what I can gather, no one lives there now except a handful of locals who get their living by fishing, and diving for coral.' People who still clung to their ancient way of life, and the peace it afforded them, and which Tara yearned to share for a while as an antidote to her customary hectic schedule of travelling and social contact. 'Nobody's going to rob me, I've got nothing to steal,' she assured Peggy airily.

'Except yourself,' her friend warned her darkly.

From the look on the face of the man striding towards her across the white sand beach, he would not be above doing that, Tara thought apprehensively. Dry sand puffed up under his decisive step, and was caught by the wind and blown in gritty clouds about his feet, making him look as if he was walking in smoke. A brown-haired Vulcan, who shouted incomprehensible instructions at her as he approached.

'Get into the cab of your vehicle, where you're safe!' He reached her and ordered her again, peremptorily, 'Get in!' He had to raise his voice and shout above the thunder of the surf, and the ever rising shriek of the wind that had torn at the island with increasing force since daylight. He raised his hand and gestured violently towards the vehicle, as if he thought she might not have heard him, or failed to understand. 'Get into the cab!'

'I'll get in when I'm good and ready!' Tara shouted back, nettled by his authoritarian attitude. 'I came out to wipe the van windows clear of sand, I can't see a thing through them with this gale blowing.'

'This is no time to be house-proud!'

The stranger stepped right up to her, and without warning he bent down and scooped her up in his arms, and ignoring her shrill protests, wrenched open the door of the caravanette, and unceremoniously dumped her into the passenger seat. Before she could gather her scattered wits, he slammed the door shut in her face, and within seconds he rounded the van and climbed into the driving seat beside her.

'Women drivers!' he mocked. 'I might have known you'd leave your key in the ignition!' It was the bigoted criticism of a pure male chauvinist, and Tara reacted explosively.

'Leave the ignition key alone, and get out of my van!' she ordered him furiously. 'What do you think . . .?'

'I think you're a lot safer in here than outside under those coconut palms.' Long fingers stilled on the ignition key, but they did not loose it. Subconsciously Tara noticed that his fingernails were clean, and cut short, fastidiously groomed in keeping with the rest of his appearance. No, he was definitely not a hippie.

Which probably made him all the more dangerous than would be a member of that unkempt and misguided band, she realised uneasily.

'From the way the wind's rocking the van, I'd feel a lot safer outside of it than in.' And safer still if she was a long distance away from this domineering intruder. 'If only I'd listened to Peggy,' she regretted. Surreptitiously she looked round her, but from the passenger seat she could not easily reach into the back of the van, and there was nothing near at hand with which she could protect herself.

Wham!

The huge green coconut bounced on to the bonnet of the van with a crash that shook the vehicle, and nearly made Tara jump out of her skin. The hapless steel bent under the force of the impact, and the coconut split into half a dozen pieces. Tara gulped, and watched wide-eyed as creamy milk from the shattered nut ran in rivulets to form a pool in the middle of the dented bonnet.

'That could easily have been your skull.'

His voice broke through the numbed shock of the shattered nut, bringing home forcefully the danger outside the van. Reminding Tara vividly of the even worse potential danger inside it, sitting right beside her, watching her with eyes. . . . She swallowed again, and a shock of a different kind transfixed her, as she stared into his eyes, dark blue like a midnight sky, with tiny lines fanning out from the corners of them, the lines marginally paler than the deep tan which covered the rest of his face, as if his eyes were used to looking at long distances, squinting against the sun. Tara blinked, and broke the shackle of his stare, and retorted defensively,

'Well, it wasn't my skull, and anyway, how was I to know coconuts aren't fixed to the tree securely?' She made it sound as if the glue had come unstuck, but no glint of humour lightened the grim expression on the stranger's face.

'It pays to find out where it's safe to stop, *before* you park up,' he told her tersely. 'When Mother Nature sends in her demolition squad, she's not fussy about what gets broken.'

'I'm aware there's a storm blowing, but along this stretch of coast they never last for long.' Haughtily Tara justified her decision to park under the palm trees.

'This storm won't blow itself out very quickly,' the intruder prophesied. 'So let's get out of here before another nut comes down, probably through the roof of the van. Where's your travelling companion?' he asked abruptly.

'What travelling companion?' She looked up at him, puzzled.

'Whoever it is you're travelling with,' he rephrased impatiently. His blue glance slid to her left hand, noted the ringless fingers, and he added un-interestedly,

'Better call him or her quickly, so that we can get out of here while we're still in one piece.'

'I haven't got a companion.' The words were out before she could stop them. Too late, Tara realised the danger of allowing this man to know she was travelling on her own. Too late she wished she had said there was a six feet tall boy-friend in the offing, and then the stranger would have climbed out of the van, and gone on his way, and icy fear clutched at her as she realised she had betrayed her aloneness and put herself at his mercy, and now he, as well as she, knew there was no help at hand if she needed it. By her own careless admission she had as good as told him he could do as he pleased, and there was no one there to prevent him.

'You mean you're travelling in this outfit on your own? You haven't even brought along a dog for

protection?' Incredulity, and surprisingly anger, flared
in the blue eyes. 'You must be mad to. . . .'

Wham!

The second coconut hit the bonnet close to the
windscreen. Tara winced away from it as if she had
been struck, but mercifully the glass remained intact.

'Time to go.'

With fluid speed the stranger fired the engine,
debraked, and wrenched the caravanette round in a
quick turn, then pointed it towards the jungle-clad
hills that rose steeply from out of the bay.

'You can't go through the jungle, there isn't a road.'
Panic took Tara by the throat at the thought of being
carried willy-nilly into the seclusion of the trees.
'Turn it round, go along the beach—I can park further
away from the palms, on the other side of the
headland.' Frantically she grasped at the wheel,
striving to turn the van parallel to the sea.

'There isn't a beach beyond the headland.' He
fended off her grasping hands with steel fingers,
steering one-handed without deviating a whit from his
intended course.

'Of course there's a beach, I came along it myself to
get here,' Tara argued hotly. 'Beyond the headland,
across that way,' she gestured to the huge bluff of rock
that ran like a serpent towards the sea, and was only
faintly visible now through clouds of wind driven
spray from the enormous combers breaking over the
outlying rocks. 'There's plenty of room to pass round
the end of the rocks.'

'Beyond that bluff of rocks, the sea's piled right in
deep to the edge of the jungle, and with this wind
driving it, it's unlikely to go down even at low tide,'
the stranger informed her tersely. 'In another hour,
with the way the wind's rising now, this beach here
will be in the same state. It's only the bluff of rock
that's protected it up to now, and I don't intend to be

around when the water comes in here as well. The beach on the other side of the bluff is like a cauldron, nothing could survive in water as wild as that,' he told her, and added grimly, 'Until I spotted your vehicle just now, I thought you were under the surface, on the other beach.'

'You thought I . . .? How did you know I was even on the island?' Tara demanded. Since the barge had dropped her and the caravanette on the island, she had seen no other living soul, not even the few islanders who were supposed to be still living on Mahila.

'One of the local fishermen came limpet-picking off the rocks on the headland yesterday, and he saw your vehicle parked under the palms, so I knew whoever owned it had to be still somewhere around, if they weren't already drowned.'

And on that information, this man had come looking for her. Why? What was his motive? Tara felt her mouth go dry, and bitterly regretted not heeding Peggy's advice and holidaying in Hawaii, tourists notwithstanding. Suddenly, masses of tourists seemed a nice, safe embellishment to the scenery. But they were on another island, a long distance away, and she was here, and heading towards the jungle, and who knew what else, at frightening speed.

'You can't go on, there isn't a road.' The unknown man presented a worse hazard than the coconuts. Of the two, Tara decided she much preferred the coconuts.

'There's a rough track through the jungle, across what's left of an abandoned sugar plantation. It's the only way.'

'The only way to where?' The caravanette rocked wildly as she tried to wrest the wheel from him and turn the vehicle back on to the beach, anywhere away from the fringe of jungle that loomed closer by the second, dark, threatening, presenting the possibility of unthinkable terrors if she should enter it in the company of the stranger. She might as well have tried to wrest the whistle from the wind. Skilfully he guided the vehicle across the sand, avoiding the outcrops of lava rock that jutted through the surface like jagged teeth, waiting to tear at the wheels should the vulnerable tyres scrape against the sharp surfaces. Desperately Tara looked round her, judging the possibility of jumping out and running for cover, but the risk was too great. She would probably end up like Peggy, with a broken ankle. At least with two whole feet, she could use them both to run away as and when the opportunity occurred.

'The only way to the leeward side of the island,' he answered her question laconically. 'All the locals are already there, gathered on a small peninsula that forms one side of the bay.'

'I came to get away from crowds, not to join them!' Somehow she must get away from this man. The risk would have to be taken. Even if his motives were as pure as the driven snow, which she doubted. . . . She slanted an apprehensive upwards glance at his face, and found nothing in its lean hardness to reassure her. She had no intention of being kidnapped by an interfering stranger, and forced against her will to join a community on the other side of the island, simply because a gale was blowing. Impulsively Tara swung round on the seat and grabbed for the door handle, lifting her feet sideways at the same time, ready to jump out the moment the door swung open.

'Stay where you are.' With quicksilver reaction the man beside her divined her intention, almost before she moved. One lean hand reached out and hooked strong fingers in the back waistband of her slacks, and held her fast.

'Let me go!' Tara exploded furiously. 'First you hijack my vehicle, and now you have the nerve to expect me to sit here meekly and allow myself to be hauled over to the other side of the island, just because there's a storm blowing!'

'Right now, the other side of the island looks a lot more attractive than this one,' he replied curtly, and hung on to her slacks.

'It's nothing but bare volcanic rock on that side of the mountain.' It was where the barge had landed Tara and the caravanette, a barren land of ancient lava flows and low scrub, admittedly warmer and drier than the windward side, but lacking the lush vegetation and exotic flowers that, to Tara, enhanced the scenery, and made the occasional shower worth enduring. The delicate perfume of a jugful of frangipani blossoms she had picked for the living quarters of the caravanette wafted about her nostrils in the front seat. If the stranger continued to drive the vehicle across the increasingly rocky terrain at this reckless rate, the jug would undoubtedly spill over, and there would be water all over the floor, and probably over her food supplies as well. 'I don't want to go to the other side of the island, I want to stay here.' Visions of the mess she would have to clear up later added exasperation to fury, and she spun round on the seat and reached out an angry hand to wrench the ignition key from the lock.

'You can't afford to be fussy about scenery, with a hurricane due to hit the island at any minute now.' He removed his fingers from the back of her slacks and fielded her hand with humiliating ease, thrusting it out of his way, and out of reach of the ignition key, with the same nonchalant contempt that he would use to knock away a pestering insect.

'Hurricane?' Tara's hand stilled, and she caught a deep breath. 'Don't lie to me about a hurricane,' she spat furiously. 'The gale's bad enough, but it isn't a . . .'

'There's a hurricane blowing out in the Pacific. They've code-named it Daisy.'

'I know there's one blowing, I heard it on the news bulletin, but it's headed out west of here. It'll miss Mahila completely, except for the gale we're getting now.' Even if she had come to a remote Pacific island, she was still in touch with the events in the outside world, and she lost no time in letting him know what she thought of his feeble deception.

'You're a mite out of date,' her companion drawled. 'When did you last hear a news bulletin?'

'We-e-ll, yesterday afternoon,' Tara admitted reluctantly.

'Things have changed since then,' the stranger informed her. 'The wind put about early this morning, and hurricane Daisy, true to her feminine appelation, has altered her mind, and her direction. She's heading this way, fast.'

'There's no need to be sarcastic,' Tara snapped, incensed by his attitude, frightened in spite of herself, and unwilling to allow it to show before the stranger. Hippies she felt she could cope with, but a hurricane, even one named Daisy, was quite another matter. If, that was, the stranger was telling the truth.

'How do I know . . .?' She stopped.

'Try listening to the radio,' he suggested drily, 'they're issuing frequent bulletins.' Competent fingers found the radio switch on the dashboard with not even a downwards glance from their owner. 'There's no need for you to take my word for it.' Abruptly he dismissed her doubts as successfully as he had her opposition. 'Listen,' he commanded, and raised his hand for silence as the radio began to crackle, reacting to the disturbed atmosphere. A programme of light music was playing, which in any other circumstances Tara would have enjoyed listening to.

'That doesn't sound like a weather bulletin to me,'

she said, bluntly sarcastic when it had continued for a minute or two.

'Hurricane warning.' An impersonal, disembodied voice stopped her, and in the speaking silence that followed, it continued ominously, 'The hurricane, code-named Daisy, which was previously heading towards the Philippines, changed direction during the early hours of this morning, and is now on direct course for the Pacific islands. It is expected to connect with the outermost islands at any time within the next few hours. Further bulletins will be issued at frequent intervals.'

The speaker repeated the warning in three languages, then the music took over again, giving the announcement a bizarre kind of unreality.

'Now do you believe me?' The stranger reached over and snapped the wireless switch shut, and Tara swallowed hard and slumped back in her seat. The outmost island—that was Mahila. She scarcely noticed the green fringe of jungle close over and around them. While her attention was diverted, they had reached the perimeter of the trees.

'It's a good job this outfit's got a four-wheel drive,' the stranger commented casually, and reached down a slim, tanned hand to the gear lever, manipulating it easily, and slowing the vehicle to a crawl along the steep upwards track that snaked ahead of them, scarcely discernible in the dim light. The change of pace brought Tara out of her trance. Now was her chance to jump free, now, while the vehicle was inching along at a snail's pace, and there was little or no chance of a broken ankle unless she was unlucky enough to fall awkwardly. But her feet and legs seemed to have acquired a strange kind of inertia, that did not need the stranger's restraining fingers in her waist band to keep them where they were, and she turned unseeing eyes on the green wall of the jungle creeping slowly past her window, while her mind assimilated what she had heard, and added to it the astonishing fact that this man, this stranger, must have walked halfway across the mountain in tropical temperatures and gale force winds, in order to reach her on the island's windward side and pluck her, an unknown, away from the direct path of the hurricane. And far from feeling grateful for his intervention, the last thing Tara felt inclined to do at the moment was to thank him.

'Daisy isn't a very appropriate name to give to anything so destructive as a hurricane,' she criticised instead, clinging with both hands to the dashboard in front of her to steady herself against the violent rocking of the vehicle as it clawed its way upwards on the diabolical surface of the track.

'Hurricanes are always given women's names,' he drawled, and for the briefest second he tooks his eyes from off the road and slanted her a glance, and Tara flushed angrily at the glimmer of amusement in his eyes.

'I don't see why,' she contested hotly.

'Because hurricanes are changeable, unpredictable, and go round in circles. And you're right,' he conceded loftily, and to Tara's chagrin his finely cut lips tilted upwards in a brief grin, 'they're destructive as well.'

'Of all the cynical, chauvinistic . . . ouch!' Her fierce condemnation ended in a groan of agony as the seat of her slacks parted company with the seat of the van, and her head cracked sharply against the cab roof. The vehicle swayed dangerously, and Tara held her breath as a particularly ferocious hole tilted it at an angle that convinced her it was about to turn over. The stranger clung grimly on to the bucking wheel, the muscles of his arms standing out like whipcord under the strain, and by a miracle the vehicle righted itself and clawed its way out of the defile, then crawled on. Tara took a deep, shaky breath.

'Why don't you look where you're going?' She used it to shout at him, unjustly because the dim light under the trees made it impossible to see the track clearly, and it was so narrow there was no space to turn aside from obstructions. Unidentified creepers scraped the windows on either side, threatening to halt its passage, and Tara knew a moment of pure panic at the prospect of the vehicle becoming stuck fast if the track should close in further still. 'I'm supposed to return the caravanette intact to the car hire company at the end of my holiday,' she reminded its driver with considerable asperity.

'If you must go adventuring on your own, you can't complain if you meet up with a few discomforts on the way,' he retorted callously, and Tara glowered at him speechlessly, too shaken by the bucking van to have any breath left to argue.

'We're coming out of the jungle now,' he added fraught minutes later, and to Tara's relief the track in front of them began to widen, and the trees fell back on either side, and the sky, and clear daylight, reappeared again. So did the gale force wind. Her relief was shortlived. The trees had sheltered them from the gale on the upwards slope, but now the green wall was below them, and the track wound on, even more execrable than before, across an exposed plateau of bare lava rock, up and up towards the summit of the long-dormant volcano.

'If we go much higher, we'll soon be in the crater itself.' She viewed the eerie moonscape terrain with fearful eyes, the weird shapes of wind-eroded rock a nightmare sculpture, broken here and there by tall, slender silver leaves of a plant that incredibly found sustenance on the red cinder cones of the extinct volcano, incongruous in their beauty among the surrounding desolation. Was the caravanette capable of taking the strain? she wondered uneasily. The wind swooped on it like an animal seeking to recapture its prey, buffeting the high sides of the vehicle with hammer blows that made the hollow rear end echo like a drum, keeping time to the frightened thudding of her heart.

'We can't go on along this track, we'll surely capsize.' The track lost itself in an old lava flow, wrinkled as an elephant's hide, and studded with boulders like sharp teeth, waiting to rend intruding wheels and tyres. It reappeared on the other side of the mass, turning back on itself in a hair-raising bend that clung precariously to the outside edge of the mountain, with barely sufficient room to take the wheels of the caravanette, let alone its bulging top sides, between the high cliffs rising on one side, and a terrifying drop on the other.

'Turn back,' Tara shouted, 'turn back, before it's too late! We'll never stay upright on a bend as sharp as that. The van's too wide. The wind's too strong. We'll be blown over the edge!' she shrieked.

Her only answer was a terse, 'Sit still, and hold tight.'

'It's suicide,' she sobbed. 'You're mad to attempt it, we'll both be killed!' He had accused her of being mad to park under coconut palms in a gale. Compared to this, her own transgression was a virtue. To go on along the track was worse than suicide, it was maniacal. And in doing so, he put her life in jeopardy, as well as his own.

'If we go back, we can shelter in the jungle.' Any risks the jungle might hold with the stranger as a companion paled into insignificance beside this. 'Turn back,' she begged him, too frightened now for pride, 'it's inviting disaster to go any further.'

He drove on. The wildly uneven surface of the lava

flow shook any further protests from Tara into teeth-chattering silence, and before she could regain her breath the van wheels found the track again on the other side of the flow, at the start of the bend. They slowed to a crawl as the path narrowed further still at the very point of the hairpin, and for a second Tara closed her eyes, but fear forced them open again. She did not dare to look, and she did not dare not to look. The coastline they had left lay like a map below them, and she stared downwards at it with horrified eyes. Boiling seas broke in fountains of spray right to the jungle edge, covering the beach where she had parked. The stranger's description of them as a cauldron was unnervingly accurate, and a shudder ran through her at the prospect of being blown off the cliff face and into the waiting maw of such a sea.

'Hold on,' he repeated shortly, and pointed the bonnet of the vehicle straight into the sharpest angle of the bend.

'No!' Tara whispered, and her hands flew to her mouth, pressing her cry back into her throat. Frozen with terror, she watched the cliff edge loom up, felt every slight bump of the approach twang at her taut nerves. Once, the tyres slid on loose shale, and she buried her face in her fingers, waiting for the end, but with a skilled twist of the wheel the driver coolly righted it, and the vehicle crept on. The wind buffeted its high sides. How could be ignore such a buffeting? Tara dragged down her hands and twisted them together in her lap, staring at him with straining eyes, but his own never faltered, they fixed themselves on the track ahead with a look of inflexible determination, as if the only thing that mattered to him in the world was to reach the point of the bend.

And once there, what then? To be hurtled into space, hundreds of feet to the rocks below, there to be ground into nothingness by the pounding surf, whose dull, animal roar could be heard even at this height, as a sinister background accompaniment to the scream of the wind? It increased in velocity as they gained the point of the hairpin, hurling itself against the sides of the caravanette, pressing the vehicle towards the sheer face of the rock rising steeply on the inside edge of the track. Dimly it dawned on Tara's paralysed mind that the stranger must have known it would press them against the rock, he had actually relied on the wind to do just that, and to push the vehicle towards safety, and not towards the edge of the cliff, and disaster. He had known, and he had allowed her to suffer the fears of the damned, without bothering to explain. It was cruel, heartless. An aeon of fear passed, then the bend was behind them and so was the wind, pressing them downwards now towards the comparative haven of the leeward shore. With a great effort Tara ungripped her hands, and winced at the livid marks left where her nails had dug deep ridges into her palms.

The change of direction did nothing to improve the surface of the track, but at least the sparse vegetation, mostly consisting of low scrub, made it possible to see around them. Something small and black and horned leapt away in front of them, startled by the unaccustomed sight of the vehicle, and its panic-stricken flight put up a small flock of birds. Tara's companion said laconically,

'Wild goat. They feed on the scrub hereabouts. The birds are a kind of quail, they feed on the berries.'

His observation was so unexpected, and so very like her own practised patter when on duty on one of her firm's long-distance touring coaches, as she briefed each current band of holidaymakers on points of interest along the route, that Tara was surprised into a laugh.

'I didn't expect a guided tour thrown in!' The laugh made her feel better. It released the tension and the terror and the sheer unbelievableness of the last few hours, in an uncontrollable burble of mirth that restored her to near normal again.

'It comes at no extra charge,' he responded with a grin, and suddenly they were laughing together, his white teeth gleamed against his tanned skin, and the monster who had hijacked her vehicle, and kidnapped her person, because a man. A disturbingly attractive man.

'What made you laugh?' His question was as unexpected as was his comment about the goat, and it startled Tara into a candid answer.

'You sounded just like me, when I've got a party of tourists aboard who want to learn all about the sights,' she told him truthfully. 'I'm a courier.'

'And what does the party of tourists call its courier?'

'Tara. Tara Brodie,' she answered promptly, and waited. For the first time, she realised she did not know the stranger's name, and suddenly it became important to her. She did not try to analyse why, she just knew that it was. Perhaps he would not reveal his true name? Perhaps he would say he was John Smith, or David Brown? She stole a look at his face, his lean, proud face, and knew he would not, knew instinctively he would scorn to use any other name than his own.

'Bryn Mathieson. Bryn to my friends.' His introduction left her in limbo, undecided whether he expected her to call him by his first name or not.

'If he thinks I'm going to call him Mr Mathieson, he's got another think coming!' Tara told herself huffily.

'And how did you get on to the island, Tara?'

That clinched it. If he took the liberty of using her first name, she would use his.

'I came on one of the barges that ferry between the islands. They put me ashore on the leeward side. There's a small landing stage in the bay, that used to belong to the sugar company, and it's still useable. I got round to the other side of the island by driving along the beaches at low tide,' she said simply. Even if she had known of the track across the mountain, she would never have summoned up the courage to tackle it on her own. Such a journey required a special kind of nerve that Tara would be the first to admit she did not possess. Remembering the boiling seas that now covered the beaches she had driven across, her mind baulked at the way in which this man had managed to reach her on foot, but independently she decided not to give him the satisfaction of questioning his route.

'How did you arrive on Mahila?' she asked him instead. She strove to make her voice indifferent, but did not quite succeed. Bryn Mathieson's presence on the island aroused her curiosity. All her previous information had led her to expect that no one except a few fishermen and their families were now resident here, and Bryn's presence came as a distinct shock, upsetting all her preconceived notions of a solitary holiday far from the maddening crowd. Bryn Mathieson was a crowd in himself, she thought edgily, and his behaviour she found maddening in the extreme.

Apart from his name, who was he? Now that the immediate danger was past, the question reasserted itself. Could he, perhaps, be an overseer of the old sugar plantation, who had remained behind when it was finally abandoned? Or even the owner, come to revisit his old property, maybe with a view to reopening operations here? Of the two, Tara favoured her companion being the owner. He had the look, the air, and certainly the authoritarian behaviour of one who was accustomed to his word being obeyed. In her case he made certain it was obeyed, and the ethics of his action apart, his success in that direction rankled badly.

'I came in the same way.'

'You weren't on the barge,' Tara challenged him swiftly. The ferry only called in at the island every other week, and she would have seen him if he had been a passenger.

'I used my own transport.' They rounded the slope of the mountain and came in sight of the bay on the other side. With a casual hand he gestured downwards, and Tara's eyes widened as she caught sight of the sleek, ocean-going yacht tossing at anchor in the heaving waters.

'Some transport!' The words were wrung from her grudging lips.

'The yacht can cope with most kinds of weather, but it isn't sensible to buck a hurricane,' he replied drily. 'I ran her into shelter in the harbour until it blows itself out.'

'Her?' She spoke abstractedly, uninterested in his answer, her mind conjuring up a vision of Bryn at the helm of his sleek craft, nursing it skilfully through the wild water, calculating the strength of his vessel, and making his judgment coolly on that basis alone, and not through any personal fear of the hurricane. Rather would he relish the challenge of the elements, testing his nerve and his skill against their fury, but strong enough not to allow his personal feelings to deflect his judgment in the best interests of his craft.

'*Roseanne.*'

'It was a second or two before his meaning penetrated. Tara had forgotten she asked him a question. Almost, she reminded him that her name was Tara, not Roseanne. Then she remembered, and her question and his answer connected, and another question beat painfully at the doors of her mind, the answer to it as important to her as had been her need to know Bryn's name.

Who was Roseanne? His wife? He spoke the name

with affection, and a strange darkness settled on Tara's spirits, and she did not want to analyse that, either. She longed to know and she feared to know the answer, and the fear won and sealed her lips and left the question unasked, while she viewed her own silence with astonished disbelief.

'What on earth's come over me?' she wondered aghast, and sought solace in her own answer, 'It must be the effect of the electricity in the atmosphere.' Bryn Mathieson had the same effect on her. He exuded the same compelling, unseen power, she could feel it now, reaching out to engulf her, sapping at her courage and destroying her powers of resistance. She took a deep, steadying breath, steeling herself to withstand the invasion of his dominant personality.

'The storm's got at me,' she told herself shakily. It was the only rational explanation for such irrational behaviour, for such a complete departure from her normally assured self that allowed this man, this stranger, to affect her as no other man had ever succeeded in doing before. Being brought up with five brothers made Tara's normal approach to the male sex a practical, hail-fellow-well-met affair that had brought her heart unscathed to the age of twenty-five. Bryn Mathieson was the first man to find a chink in her armour. Disconcertingly, he widened it.

'That's how I came to be on the island, and how I learned you were here too.' To both of them the island had represented a haven, for different reasons, but it was rapidly threatening to become just the opposite for herself, Tara thought uneasily. Bryn Mathieson was fast becoming a greater danger to her peace of mind than the hurricane was to her physical safety. At no little risk to himself he had crossed the island to her side to pluck her from the path of the approaching danger, and remorse pricked her for her previous lack of gratitude.

'I suppose I ought to thank you for coming to fetch me, before the hurricane hits us,' she forced out reluctantly, and was startled by the flash of pure amusement that lit her companion's eyes.

'There's no need to thank me,' he disclaimed airily. 'I didn't cross the island on purpose to rescue you. I came because I needed your caravanette.'

CHAPTER TWO

HE came because he needed her caravanette! Not because of any altruistic motive, not gallantly to rescue a damsel in distress, but because, for his own selfish reasons, he wanted her vehicle. Which he had promptly taken with a total disregard for the rights of ownership! His effrontery left Tara speechless, but not for long.

'You ... wanted ... my ... caravanette?' she ground out slowly, as if by saying it out loud she might the better comprehend the incomprehensible, believe the explanation that grew with frightening clarity in her mind, and which she most urgently did not want to believe.

Bryn had come ashore from his yacht, which she could plainly see heaving up and down on the storm-tossed surface of the bay, well clear of the inshore coral reef. In such wild water it would be impossible for him to return to his cabin for the night, which neatly left him stranded without sleeping accommodation.

'You're not sleeping in my van!' she stormed angrily. Indignation struck sparks from her eyes, and she rounded on him furiously. 'Just because there are two bunks in there, it doesn't give you the right to occupy the other one!'

If he chose to do so, she realised uneasily, there was absolutely nothing she could do to prevent him. His lean, hard six feet plus of athlete's frame told her plainly enough that she would be no match for his superior strength if she should try to throw him out. But if she failed, where was she herself to sleep? Unless.... An icy hand clutched at her as her thoughts progressed. Unless Bryn expected her to sleep in the van with him? Bitterly she remembered her airy assurance to Peggy,

'I've got nothing to steal.'

And her friend's dark warning, 'Except yourself.'

Bryn had already stolen her thoughts, but that was as far as she intended him to go. With mounting rage she opened her mouth to tell him so.

'I don't want your caravanette for my own use.' His eyes laughed at her, deriding her for her suspicions; scorning her for her fears, and jeering at her for her inability to do anything about it if he should choose to justify them.

'Then what . . . who . . .?'

'There's a baby due to be born at any time now, and an open beach in the middle of a hurricane isn't the best place for it to arrive,' he explained succinctly.

'Whose baby?' Could it be Roseanne's? Unaccountably Tara felt sick. So many questions, most of them unanswered, and all to do with this man, who a few short hours ago she did not know existed. Now she did know, and knew too, with a helpless sense of inevitability, that those few short hours would change the course of her life.

'The wife of one of the island's residents. They saw me come ashore, and invited me to join them when they knew the hurricane was coming. It's the least I can do, to try to help them now.'

The wife of one of the island's residents. . . . Relief washed over Tara, an immense tidal wave of relief that rocked her mentally off balance, and left her bruised and shaken as if she had been engulfed by one of the huge white-tipped combers that buffeted the beach below them. She felt the colour drain from her cheeks, and her ears sang with a dizziness that made her lean limply back in her seat. Vaguely she heard Bryn's voice.

'Don't you like heights?' She blinked him back into focus, and became aware that he was looking at her keenly with those deep blue eyes of his, that probed her dizziness and noted her pallor, and mercifully put the wrong construction on both. 'Close your eyes if it makes you feel queasy,' he suggested, 'although the track's quite safe from here on, we'll soon be down on the lower slopes of the mountain.'

It was not the height, or the track, or anything else about the mountain that made her feel queasy, but Bryn was not to know that. Tara cringed from the thought of what he would say if she told him the real reason for her pallor. What, indeed, would she tell him? She hardly knew the reason herself. Her mind struggled in a whirlpool of confusion that equalled the boiling seas below them. Gratefully she followed his advice and closed her eyes, and discovered too late that his piercing blue stare penetrated her lowered lids with disconcerting ease, the blinding darkness of them making her even more vividly attuned to his presence beside her than she was before. Small evidences of his presence impinged upon her heightened senses. His seat creaked slightly as he moved in it, manipulating the driving mechanism. It never protested when she drove the van, her slight frame barely making any impression on the upholstery, let alone moving the seat. She felt the gear-change in the altered rhythm of the vehicle, and the movement of his hand upon the lever brought his arm into brief contact with her own. It was a slight, light brushing together of their arms, and then it was gone, but its effect was as if another comber had rolled in over her, bowling her off her feet again just as she was beginning to pick herself up from the first. She shrank back against her seat lest he should change gear again, lest his arm should touch her own again, and another comber should drown her altogether in this new, bewildering turbulence of emotion that was more frightening than anything that had happened during the last few hours, more frightening than the hurricane to come, and quite beyond her powers to cope with. Her heart beat like a living pain against her side, and above its uneven throb she could hear the sigh of her own breathing, shallow, unsatisfying gasps for air that did nothing to ease the turbulence, and made the pain worse.

'You can open your eyes, we're on level ground now.'

Metaphorically speaking, she was on anything but level ground, Tara thought raggedly, but she opened her eyes, and immediately they widened in alarm as she viewed the beach where the barge had landed her the day before. As the beach she knew it was unrecognisable. The landing stage had disappeared beneath curling green combers as high as a house, that hurled themselves shorewards as if intent on destroying the island itself, to meet the latter's line of defence in a stickleback spine of rocks that exploded the combers with a constant, sullen booming sound, and showers of flying spray. Bryn reached out a hand to the controls, and the twin windscreen wipers began a rhythmic passage across the glass in front of her, mute measure of the force of the wind that carried the spray to blot out their vision even at this distance from the shoreline.

'Where are the fishermen and their families? I thought you said....' Tara probed the beach with suspicious eyes. There were rocks, and storm debris, and flying spray, but of human beings there was no sign. She turned accusing eyes on her companion. 'I can't see anybody here.'

'They're gathered in the shelter of that wall of rock halfway up the beach, out of reach of the wind and the spray. I'm told it's an ancient sheltering place when there's a bad storm blowing. The people simply abandon their homes on the other side of the island, and wait here until it blows over.'

'Time doesn't matter out here,' Tara exclaimed
enviously. 'The people surely must have a link with
Spain somewhere, their attitude is so exactly like the
Spanish *mañana*.'

'And the exact opposite to ours,' Bryn agreed
ruefully. 'We could usefully take a lesson from them.
We shall probably have to,' he added soberly. 'The
seas are getting worse by the minute, and even after
the hurricane's blown itself out, it'll take a while
before they calm down sufficiently to make them
navigable again. The locals know that, they've brought
their canoes well up on to the rocks, out of reach if
there's an exceptionally high tide.' He gestured ahead,
and through the blinding spray Tara caught sight of a
line of outrigger canoes drawn high up towards a long
wall of black rock that curled strangely like an arm at
the base of the mountain, between it and the sea.
People moved in its shelter, Tara could see one or two
children playing as they moved in closer.

'It's like a little inland harbour.' She gazed at it
fascinated. 'I didn't notice it when I landed.'

'From the shore it looks to be part of the mountain,'
Bryn commented. 'It's an ancient lava flow,' obligingly
he continued his impromptu guided tour. 'The cooling
lava piled up against a line of rocks already jutting out
of the sand, and solidified into the wall of rock you can
see now.'

'It makes an ideal shelter from the wind,' Tara
remarked appreciatively. Even here, on the leeward
side of the island, the gale had reached proportions to
be reckoned with, and was growing stronger by the
minute. It rocked the caravanette in a manner that
made her thankful they were not still on the summit of
the mountain, then the buffeting lessened, and Bryn
drew the vehicle to a halt in the shelter of the rock
wall, so they could speak again without having to raise
their voices to make themselves heard.

'Here's Paul.'

A young man detached himself from a group of people clustered close to the base of the wall, and walked towards them. He was shorter than Bryn, but he possessed the splendid physique of the pure Polynesian, a young, brown-skinned god of the islands, with a pleasant smile and a cheerful greeting, and a word of unexpected thanks for Tara.

'It's more than kind of you to allow my wife to use your caravanette. The hurricane couldn't have come at a worse time for Meli and me.'

'Snap!' Tara thought bitterly. The wandering hurricane could not have chosen a worse time for her, either. And as for allowing his wife to use the vehicle, Bryn gave her no choice in the matter. He crossed the island with every intention of commandeering it, and gave his reason for doing so, only as an afterthought on the way down from the mountain. She could feel his eyes on her now, watching her, waiting for her reaction to the newcomer's thanks. Testing her, she sensed uneasily. For what? Was he silently daring her to refuse the newcomer? Refuse the man's wife, in her extremity?

The temptation to refuse was great, to deny Bryn the spoils of his piracy. If he had taken her vehicle for his own use, she would have denied him with all the strength at her command, leaving him to brave the storm on the beach rather than allow him to take advantage of the admittedly flimsy shelter the van provided. But deny a mother-to-be, and her not-yet child? No, it was impossible. Tara's warm-hearted nature recoiled from the mere suggestion, and unconsciously she shook her head. Instantly the man's face clouded.

'But I thought ... Bryn said....' He stopped, obviously embarrassed, and Tara felt Bryn stiffen by her side. She looked at the speaker, puzzled by his dismay, then the explanation for it dawned upon her.

'But of course you must use my van,' she cried impulsively, and the young husband's smile returned. 'Tell Bryn where best to park it, and I'll help your wife to settle in right away.' She had done two things at once, that gave her immense satisfaction. She had manoeuvred Bryn into a position where he had no option but to comply with her wishes to park the van, and she had effectively put him outside it while she joined with the young wife in the strictly woman's world of preparing for the new arrival.

'I'll park it for you.' To Tara's chagrin, Paul held out his hand for the ignition key, thus neatly letting Bryn out of her trap. And dropping her into one of her own making if she was not quick, she realised nervously.

'I'll come with you.' She turned hurriedly to re-enter the van.

'It's hardly worth it, it's only a few yards to where I need to park it, and it'll be bumpy going across the rocks,' Paul demurred. 'Better to stay here with Bryn—I won't be a moment, then I'll come back and introduce you to my wife.'

It was definitely not better from her point of view to remain with Bryn, but for the sake of a ride of a few yards she could not climb back into the van beside Paul without making herself look foolish. Reluctantly Tara forced her feet to remain fixed to the rock she was standing on, and Paul set the van rolling, while Bryn drawled provocatively,

'Nice of you to offer him the use of your van.'

Did he imagine she was hard-hearted enough to refuse it? Or did he think she had not the courage? The possibility that it might be the latter put an edge to Tara's voice, and she snapped,

'I couldn't refuse it in the circumstances, nobody would. I just don't like my belongings being hijacked without a by-your-leave, that's all.' And herself as well, but she did not feel inclined to press that point.

'There was no time for explanations, and as for hijacking your vehicle, I took the trouble to cross the island to do you a favour,' he told her curtly.

'Do *me* a favour?' Her voice rose indignantly. 'All I wanted was to be left alone, in peace!'

'Yes, you.' His voice was harsh, growling a warning that she had gone far enough. 'When the hurricane hits us, you'll have cause to be thankful you're on this side of the island, and not on the windward side, and more thankful still that you've got company.'

'It depends upon the company.' Her tone implied his was less than welcome.

'We're very glad to have yours.' Paul's return put an end to the argument that was rapidly degenerating into a quarrel. 'I've parked the van as close to the rock as it'll go,' he assured her, 'but just the same I'll rope it as well as an extra precaution.'

'I'll help you,' Bryn offered.

'I'll come and start to prepare the inside.' Tara refused to allow Bryn to interfere with the internal arrangements, whatever he did to the exterior.

'Come and meet my wife first,' Paul invited, and taking Tara by the arm he walked her between himself and Bryn towards the small group gathered under the rock wall. 'Meli, come and meet Tara.'

She was lovely, with the long, raven-haired, dark-eyed loveliness of the islands. Tara felt her own short dark hair and hazel eyes, with the tiny gold flecks in them that burned when she became angry, pale in comparison with the dusky beauty of the girl who rose rather heavily to her feet to greet them.

'I'm so grateful for your help.' Her voice was attractively husky and her smile and handclasp were warm, and gazing at her Tara mourned the fact that she was a courier and not an artist, with the talent to commit such beauty to canvas, and tried to convince herself that it was her lack of talent in that direction that forced the sharp sigh from her lips, while she knew deep down that it was another lack, more fundamental than that of art, that brought a strange ache to her throat on the breath of the sigh, and made her own voice as husky as Meli's as she replied sincerely,

'I'm glad I happened to be here.'

She wondered how it was that Paul and Meli were here, seeming content to live in this isolated spot so far from the mainstream of life on the other islands, while their voices and their manner betrayed education, and a different mode of living from that of the simple fisher-folk. But such a question could not be asked, so she had to content herself with silence, and invited instead,

'Come and see the van.' She lent a steadying hand to help Meli to negotiate the step into the living quarters at the back of the vehicle.

'I'll be glad when I've got junior in my arms,' the mother-to-be confessed ruefully as she eased herself on to the nearest bunk and settled her cumbersome body, that Tara sensed was once as lissom as her own. Would soon be again. One glance was sufficient to tell her that Meli's wish would shortly be granted.

'He couldn't have chosen a lovelier spot to arrive in, though his timing's a bit inconvenient,' Tara smiled.

'You must be wondering why we've chosen to have him here, on Mahila, and not in a nice hygienic hospital in Hawaii,' Meli observed shrewdly, and Tara felt her colour rise.

'It's not my business,' she protested, and wished, not for the first time, that her mobile face would not reveal her thoughts so easily.

'You're bound to think it strange,' Meli persisted, 'but our reason's quite simple really. We want our child to have a *real* childhood, and grow up with real values, and not be pressurised by the synthetic ones of the rat-race that has taken over much of the world we knew. Oh, it's not just an airy-fairy dream,' she read the doubt in Tara's expression. 'Our child won't lack education. Paul and I are both teachers. In fact, I run a school for the children of the fishermen here, it occupies my time while I'm waiting.'

'It sounds idyllic,' Tara agreed.

'It's practical as well,' Meli returned seriously. 'Education shouldn't just come from books. It comes from a whole way of life, from the forest, and the mountain, the wind and the sea, which all combine to build an inner strength, a self-reliance that can't be gained from formal education.' She warmed to her theme, and her enthusiasm caught at Tara's imagination. 'When our child is old enough to go out into the world, we want him to have that strength,' she finished quietly.

'But if he has no knowledge of the outer world?' By common consent, they both spoke of Meli's child as a boy.

'Oh, but he will have,' Meli spoke confidently. 'He'll travel, along with Paul and me, and learn about the outer word, so that he can compare the two, and judge for himself. Paul has to make frequent trips among the islands to research material for his book,' she explained.

'I thought you said your husband was a teacher?'

'So he was ... is,' Meli corrected herself with a smile. 'But a teacher with an absorbing interest in the history of the Hawaiian people and their islands. He was in constant demand to lecture on the subject, and one day someone from a publishing company in Vancouver heard him talk, and he was so impressed he commissioned Paul there and then to write a book about it. It's such a vast subject that it'll probably run into several volumes, and several years' work,' she predicted happily. 'But the islands are changing fast, and the material needs to be gathered now, before it's too late. Before all the evidence of our folklore and culture has been flattened by the bulldozers in the crazy urge to "develop" every square inch of land for commercial profit, and our music and art debased in the name of tourism.' Briefly her husky voice became bitter.

'You mean grass skirts and guitars, and garlands of flowers?' Tara felt a prick of conscience for being part of the despised tourism.

'Something like that.' Meli laughed with a sudden change of mood. 'Though I'm not against using those things to interest visitors.' She smiled at Tara's look of surprise. 'They're part of our heritage, after all,' she shrugged, 'and tourism is an important slice of the islands' economy, they would be much poorer without it, culturally as well as financially. And it's good for people to travel and to get to know one another's way of life. But these things are only a very small part of the whole, the icing on the cake, as it were, and it's the whole in which Paul's interested, to record it for posterity before it gets irretrievably lost. And talking of time,' she checked the flood of her dissertation and gazed across anxiously at Tara, 'I wonder how long it'll be before. . . .'

'According to the latest news bulletin, we've got at most a couple of hours before the hurricane hits us,' Paul's voice remarked from outside the van.

'Men!' Meli exclaimed. 'As if I care about an old hurricane. I was meaning. . . .'

'You'll care about the hurricane if we don't get the van roped in time,' her husband's voice retorted. 'The van isn't a cradle, remember. If it rocks, it'll probably rock right over. Throw a rope across the top to me, Bryn, I'll belay it round one of these rocks here.'

'Coming across!'

Bryn's voice came across loud and clear, and from immediately behind her. Tara jerked round on her bunk and her breath expelled in a sharp hiss as her eyes met on level with his, staring in at her through the side window of the van, disconcertingly close, and piercingly blue. For a second or two she sat transfixed, unable to move, unable to look away.

Why did Bryn have to choose to work on this side of the van? she asked herself desperately. Why hadn't Meli sat on this bunk, instead of the other one? Why . . .? Confused, and dismayed by her own confusion, she tore her gaze away and slid hurriedly to her feet, turning her back to the window, still feeling Bryn's stare tingle along the length of her spine, paralysing in its intensity.

'Would you like a cup of tea?' It was the first thing that came into her head. In the spartan interior of the caravanette, with unbreakable crock mugs instead of china, it sounded trite, and somehow silly, but her scattered wits were incapable of anything better.

'How very English!' Meli laughed. 'But yes, please, I'd love one. I prefer tea to coffee.'

'Make that four cups,' Paul's voice begged plaintively from outside. 'Roping a van's thirsty work.'

'It's lucky this flower vase dropped on to the floor, instead of spilling over the supplies cupboard,' Tara remarked tartly, 'or there wouldn't have been either fit to offer you.' She bent and retrieved the empty flower vase from where it had rolled under the opposite bunk, and gathered up the faded frangipani blossoms, unforgivingly blaming Bryn for their untimely demise, while her mind registered a warning that any conversation inside the van could be clearly heard on the outside if the listener happened to be close enough to its thin metal walls.

'I'll put the kettle on,' Meli offered.

'You put the cups out,' Tara diverted her hastily,

'I'll see to the kettle. It needs to be filled, and the water container's much too heavy for you to lift.' She ducked under the tiny sink to pull it out.

'In that case, I'll pick it up for you.'

The sound of Bryn's voice brought Tara out from under the sink at speed, in dire risk of cracking her head on its underside. She had not heard him come up the steps and enter the van. She thought he was still outside, helping Paul with the ropes. She rocked back on her heels and stared up at him. His tall frame seemed to fill the van. He had to duck his head to stand under the roof, and the narrow middle aisle disappeared behind his broad shoulders.

'Let me take the water container.' He reached down, and Tara hastily let go of the handle, then he hooked two nonchalant fingers round it and lifted it out from under the sink, a feat that took the combined strength of both her own hands, even when the container was only half full.

'You're going to need more water than this.' Bryn surveyed the container with a measuring look.

'It's full to the brim,' Tara objected. She gripped the edge of the sink and pulled herself to her feet, clinging on to her support with urgent fingers to aid legs that suddenly felt uncertain beneath her. 'I only need a kettle full of water to make a pot of tea.' She wished Bryn would move away and leave her to go about her task. With him standing in the aisle, she was hemmed in between him and the low bulkhead of the cab behind her. There was no room to pass round him, and she felt trapped, and rising panic brought an almost uncontrollable urge to shout at him to move away and let her out, that had nothing to do with claustrophobia, and everything to do with his unnerving closeness and the mesmeric power of his deep blue stare.

'Where's your kettle?' he wanted to know, mercifully looking away from her to search for the utensil.

'Here.' With an immense effort she controlled the urge to shout, and rummaged in the opposite cupboard and brought out the kettle and held it up to him.

'Hold it still.'

He asked the impossible. If her life depended upon it, Tara decided raggedly, she could not stop her hands from shaking. The lid of the kettle clattered like a castinet against its side.

'Give it to me.' He took it from her impatiently and set it on the stove and dispensed water from the container in a steady stream that wasted not a single drop.

'I'll top up the container, there's a fresh water spring flowing from out of the rock a couple of yards away from the van. I'll show you.' It was less of an offer than an instruction to accompany him, but for the moment Tara felt incapable of arguing.

'All mod con laid on.' Sarcasm helped to pull her together, and she put a match to the portable gas stove, and followed Bryn down the van steps with creditable steadiness.

'Thank goodness, yes,' Bryn replied crisply. 'Though this container full won't be sufficient.'

'It holds all I need, just a kettleful at a time.'

'You'll need a good deal more, I imagine, before the night's out,' he jerked his head significantly back in the direction of the van, where Meli had come to the top of the steps to talk to Paul.

'That's Paul's problem, not mine,' Tara shrugged, not pretending to misunderstand him.

'This is a woman's job, not a man's,' Bryn retorted, and Tara blinked.

'Not this woman's job, it isn't,' she dissociated herself firmly from the coming event. 'I'm a courier, not a midwife. If Paul's got cold feet, then he must get one of the fishermen's wives to help him, there are several of them who've got children of their own.'

'I think Paul would prefer your educated ignorance to the traditional outlook of the fishermen's wives,' Bryn responded drily.

'Surely you're not serious?' One glance at his face assured her he was. It jolted her to a halt in her tracks, and she stared up at him incredulously. 'You can't really expect me to ... oh, no, this is too much!' she cried angrily. 'First you take over my caravanette for a maternity ward, and now you actually have the nerve to expect me to staff it! Nothing doing,' she refused him flatly. 'If you want to play doctor yourself, go ahead, but count me out.' She spun on her heel away from him, back towards the van.

'You can't leave another woman in the lurch at a time like this.' With a swift movement Bryn dropped the water container on to the rocks at his feet. Tara heard it drop with a dull, plastic-sounding thud, then his hands reached out and grasped her, his fingers circling her arms above the elbows with a grip that made her gasp as he swung her back to face him.

'You can't leave Meli stranded,' he grated harshly.

'Just watch me!' The pain of his merciless grip; the impossible demand he placed upon her; panic at the possibility of what the next few hours might hold if she gave in to that demand; and Bryn's sheer overwhelming strength as he pulled her to him and held her against him while his eyes bored down into her face, snapped the thin bond of Tara's sorely tried self-control, and she began to struggle frantically to free herself. Careless of the nearby presence of Paul and Meli, she raised her voice and shouted against the wind,

'Loose me! Loose....' With beating hands and kicking feet she strove blindly to make him loose her.

'Be quiet!' His shake rattled the teeth in her head and drove her breath from her lungs, cutting off her rising hysteria as effectively as a douche of cold water.

'Anyone would think I was trying to abduct you!' he growled savagely.

'Well, didn't you? Haven't you?' Her eyes blazed up at him with the helpless fury of an animal caught inescapably in a trap, the gold flecks in them glowing like tiny fires with the force of her anger. 'You drag me here against my will, then dare to accuse me of leaving Meli stranded!' She choked on the effrontery of his accusation. 'Their own high-minded notions of leaving the rat-race and getting away from it all to lead the simple life have left her stranded, not me,' she blazed. 'Paul shouldn't have brought her here in the first place if he can't take the consequences of his own actions. Now it's come to the crunch, they've no right to involve other people!' Furiously she justified her stand.

'Just the same,' Bryn bent his head until his face was a mere inch above her own. A detached part of her mind noticed the fine creases like small, pale valleys fanning out through the deep tan from the corners of his eyes. The creases would close up when he smiled, as well as when he squinted against the sun, leaving an even, all over tan. There was no sun shining in the sky now, and Bryn was definitely not smiling.

'Just the same. . . .' His face was grim and set, and there was an edge on his voice that sounded curiously like contempt. It cut like a lash, and Tara flinched, but courageously she stood her ground.

'I won't be forced into this,' she asserted stoutly. It was all very well for Bryn. He was a man, and was therefore not expected to get involved. All that was required of him was to sit on the sidelines and wait for the announcement, then offer his congratulations. It was she, Tara, who would be in the thick of the fray, coping with she knew not what. Her courage sank several notches lower when she remembered this was Meli's first baby. What if . . .? The awful possibilities

confronting her stiffened her resistance, and she faced
Bryn with set determination in her uptilted chin.

'I won't. . . .' she began defiantly.

'Tara! Tara, please come quickly. . . .'

'That's Meli.' The cry from the van spun them both
round.

'Tara!'

That was Paul, and the desperation in his voice
galvanised Bryn into action. 'Come on, there's
something beginning to happen already!'

He reached down and grabbed Tara by the hand, and
before she had time to voice the rest of her sentence
she found herself pulled along beside him, impelled
towards the fearful unknown in the caravanette, when
her every inclination was to run as fast as her feet
would carry her, in the opposite direction.

CHAPTER THREE

THE baby and the hurricane coincided.

Tara was never sure afterwards which had the most impact on her. Bryn had immediate impact. They reached the caravanette at a run which left Tara breathless and panting, but he gave her no respite. He loosed her hand and grasped her round the waist, his fingers spanning her slender measurements with a mighty grip that lifted her clear of the steps, and dumped her bodily straight inside the van.

'Get on with it, and don't argue,' he ordered her brusquely. 'I'm going back to fetch the water container.'

'Don't go. Bryn. . . .' But he was gone, and she was on her own, and fear of she knew not what closed her throat against the rest of her cry.

'Stay with me, Tara.' A soft hand reached out from the nearby bunk, and Meli clung to her fingers, anchoring her to the spot so that she could not run to follow Bryn. Convulsively Tara gripped the other girl's hand in return, as in need of reassurance as she, but she found no comfort in Meli's hold. It was weak, and clinging, and as fearful as her own, and she desperately needed that other hand to hold, from which a few short minutes ago she had fought to free herself, the strong, hard masculine grip that pulled her against her will into a situation from which it was impossible to extricate herself, and now Meli was clinging to her, depending upon her, and she had not the first notion of what to do.

'Here's the water container, nicely topped up. Have you got saucepans, or something else as well as the kettle, that will boil water?' Bryn was back, issuing crisp instructions, taking charge, the drawl in his voice not evident in his actions. He seemed to do six things at once, and expect her to do the same, while burning resentment warred with relief at his return, and the relief won that he was here, in the kitchenette, rummaging in the cupboards to find what he needed of her utensils.

'The shelf underneath the sink,' Tara directed him automatically. 'Let me see to it,' she begged. At least she knew how to boil water.

'You stay with Meli'. He found what he wanted, and selected the two largest saucepans.

'I don't know what to do!' she wailed desperately.

'You don't have to do anything, except wait.' Briefly Bryn ceased operations and swung round to face her, and she stared back at him dumbly. Her dry throat felt incapable of speech, and her hands shook so much that even if he had given her the utensils, she would have spilled more water than she boiled.

'The baby will manage everything quite well for himself,' he told her calmly. His look was piercing, daring her to turn tail. His tone was bracing, his words matter-of-fact, and his presence in the van poured new strength into her shaking limbs. 'All that you'll be required to do is to welcome the new arrival into the world, smack his backside to make him yell, then tidy up after him.'

Subconsciously, it registered with Tara that Bryn, too, spoke as if the new arrival would be a boy.

'You make it sound simple.' She recovered sufficient poise to be sarcastic. 'Since all we've got to do is to wait, we might as well have that cup of tea.'

'Make one for Paul, he could do with a bracer.' Briefly a grin flashed across Bryn's face, and he made for the van door.

'Don't go. Don't leave me here on my own!' The

panic returned in a rush and without thinking Tara reached out and grabbed him by the arm.

'I'm not going far.' Firmly he removed her clinging fingers. 'I'm going to give Paul the water container to fill up again at the spring. A job will keep his mind off his problems.'

The immediate problems were more her own than Paul's, Tara thought worriedly, but quick sympathy kept her silent as the young husband came up the van steps to take the water container from Bryn. His good-looking face was creased with anxiety, and it looked as if his dreams of leading the simple life had all suddenly turned into nightmares. He was in the same pitiable state of nerves as she was herself, and Meli was little better. Of the four of them, Bryn was the only one who seemed unaffected, and Tara followed him with questioning eyes. Was he really as confident as he seemed, or—an unexpected pang shot through her as the thought took her unawares—or was he simply uncaring?

'Top up the container with water, then come back and have your cup of tea,' he bade Paul cheerfully, and when the young husband disappeared on his errand he shot an unexpected question at Tara.

'What's the state of your battery?' he asked abruptly.

'My . . . battery?' His question did not even register on her bemused brain. He might have spoken in another language, for all the sense it made to her.

'You're going to need light, as well as water.' He spoke impatiently, and for the first time Tara realised how dark it had become. Automatically she glanced at her watch, and frowned. It must have stopped. The hands showed late afternoon, too early for it to be dark. She put the face to her ear, then realised how silly it was to expect to hear the instrument's almost inaudible tick above the rising scream of the wind.

'Give me your keys, I'll start the van engine!' Bryn had to shout to make himself heard, even in the confines of the van.

'We can't take the van anywhere until you untie the ropes,' Tara shouted back.

'I want to start the engine, not run the van. If the engine's running, it'll keep the battery charging. You never know for how long. . . .'

Crash!

'Tara, help me!'

Torrential rain tore across the roof of the van with the force of an explosion, driven by a gust of wind that made the preceding gale seem like a zephyr by comparison. The van keeled over at a sickening angle, and Meli screamed.

'We're going over!' Tara grabbed at the nearest support, and encountered Bryn.

'We'll stay upright, the ropes will hold.' He put her back on to her feet again, and she prayed he was as confident as he sounded. She envied him and loathed him for his sublime confidence, and leaned on the strength of it without compunction.

'The mountain's sheltering us from the worst force of the wind,' he added.

Then goodness help the other side of the mountain, Tara shuddered. The windward side, from which Bryn had plucked her. Where she had parked in blissful ignorance under the shelter of the coconut palms. By this time there would not be a nut left hanging, even if the palm trees themselves were still standing. The rain hammering on the roof sounded as if each individual drop was as large as a coconut, and as hard and heavy. It was less of a noise than an assault on the eardrums, and Tara longed to stuff her hands over her ears and bury her head under a pillow, and stay there until it was all over.

'Tara!' It was impossible to hear Meli's cry. Tara

saw the other girl open her mouth and call her name, twisting on the bunk in her anguish. She was dimly conscious of Paul's face, streaming with wet at the doorway. Supremely conscious of Bryn's hands, holding her, propelling her towards the bunk. She hated those hands. She hated Bryn. Every nerve of her longed to fight free from his grip, from this awful responsibility that he was thrusting upon her, but she might as well pit her puny strength against the hurricane as against his hands, that forced her inexorably forward, to face something that frightened her even more than the elements.

The hour that followed was a nightmare of confusion. The wind screamed with demonic force, striving to destroy the van. The rain battered on its roof until it seemed as if the metal must be pockmarked with dents from the force of it. Accompanying the noise from the wind and the rain, a constant booming like a battery of anti-tank guns added its quota to the cacophony of sound, as the wind drove the surf to destruction on the rocks. The whole tremendous orchestration of the storm battered at her senses, destroyed her hearing, rendered her voice useless. Bryn seemed to be everywhere at once. Just the man for an emergency, Tara told herself sarcastically, and felt a sneaking gratitude for the strength of his presence, then felt angry with herself for being grateful. It was Bryn who should be grateful to her, for being here. He had pitchforked her into a situation that was none of her seeking, and without conscience she used him, determined to make him pay the price for her services.

'More water.'

She derived vindictive satisfaction from seeing him bent double, battling against the terrific gusts of wind as he struggled towards the spring with the water container. She grabbed it out of his hand when he returned, used some, slopped a lot more, and gave him the container back again.

'More water.'

Remorselessly she drove him out again into the elements, enjoying the sight of him squelching back soaked to the skin, with his hair plastered flat against his head from the torrential downpour. She was as wet as he was, but from perspiration, not from the rain. The heat and the humidity, and the constant hissing gas jets as they boiled kettle after kettle full of water on the tiny stove, turned the van into something resembling an oven. Tara's hair stuck to her forehead, and her clothes plastered themselves flat against her body in a clammy embrace from the perspiration that ran off her in rivulets, sapping her strength until she felt ready to drop with exhaustion. And it was all Bryn's fault, she blamed him bitterly.

'La-a-a-h!'

The baby did not wait for his backside to be slapped. He let out a lusty yell of protest in competition with the noisy, inhospitable world in which he found himself, a thin, reedy cry that cut across the booming of the surf, defied the rattle of the rain, and triumphed above the scream of the wind.

'It's a boy!'

Tara had to mouth the words, but Meli understood. Her lovely dark eyes glowed and she held up her arms, mutely entreating, and Tara lifted her son and gently placed him where he belonged, in the crook of his mother's arm, and as she relinquished her tiny burden and leaned back limply, watching the two of them together, a strange feeling took possession of her.

Envy? No, it was not that. This child belonged to Meli and Paul. Longing, then? That did not quite fit, either. Tara stared down at the tiny, crumpled face, like a flower bud, still unformed, but with the promise there of beauty to come, and unconsciously she shook her head. No, it was not longing, either. Rather was it an emptiness inside her, an unexplainable ache for she knew not what. The baby's tiny face wavered and faded, and Tara blinked and drew back sharply as the clean-cut lines of Bryn's face superimposed themselves between her vision and the child. Bryn, who now the emergency was over had gone to sit on the step of the van alongside Paul, but whose features were clear in front of her eyes, his deep blue stare looking up at her in place of the limpid darkness of the baby's eyes. She put up trembling fingers and rubbed them across her forehead.

'I'm seeing things. It must be the heat, or tiredness, or. . . .' It was like a mirage in the desert. But wasn't a mirage something conjured up by the mind because it longed for whatever form the mirage took, like food, or water, or an oasis promising journey's end after years of barren searching? And why did her mind think years, when surely it should have been miles?

'Paul?' Meli's voice was faint, but it drew her husband instantly to her side. The tidying up was done. Tara did not recollect doing it, but the baby and Meli were comfortable, both of them on the verge of sleep. 'It's a boy, Paul.' Meli reached out a tender hand to her husband, and two things dawned upon Tara's tired mind. Although Meli's husky voice was low with weariness, she could hear her words without difficulty. The wind had died to a whine, the night was past and the hurricane with it. And—Tara looked at the young parents, lost in each other and their child—she was very much de trop in her own caravanette. A wave of desolation hit her and she turned her back on the scene of domestic felicity and leaned wearily against the doorpost, as Bryn rose from the step and stood tall beside her.

Except for the fact that his clothes were still soaking wet from the storm, he showed no sign that the events of the night had tired him. Whereas she herself felt bone weary, and mentally and physically drained, and probably looked it, her disgruntled thoughts assured her, Bryn looked as fresh and alert as if he had enjoyed a good night's sleep. She would not readily forgive him for the events of last night, she told herself wrathfully. She felt in dire need of a bath and a long sleep, and neither presented themselves as immediate possibilities while Paul was with Meli, which did nothing to assuage her anger against Bryn.

'Don't go in there, at least, not yet,' she warned him, unrepentantly glad to have a valid excuse to keep him out of the van. She glanced behind her and hastily looked away again, feeling an intruder on the young couple's tender embrace. 'Paul and Meli. . . .' She stopped, embarrassed.

'Congratulations seem to be in order,' Bryn observed drily, 'and since I'm debarred from offering them to the proud parents. . . .'

He offered his congratulations to Tara instead, with seeking lips that found her own and closed over them, pressing them gently but firmly back against her teeth, while his hands lifted her down across the van step to stand in front of him.

It was as if the hurricane blew all over again, only this time it raged inside her, battering at her senses until she staggered, as Bryn had staggered against the wind when fetching water from the spring, but where his strength triumphed over its fury, Tara felt herself blown hopelessly off course. Her reaction had been unnerving enough when their arms accidentally brushed against one another in the van, but this was infinitely worse. Fear gripped her as a wave of emotion such as she had never experienced before rolled over her, engulfing her, intense, overwhelming, yet leaving her feeling vitally alive. The tiredness and the desolation vanished, and a sense of helplessness enveloped her as her traitorous lips parted under the pressure of his kiss, moving murmurously with a life of their own in a response that was beyond her power to control.

Slight though it was Bryn felt the movement, and he reacted with quicksilver speed. His hands left her arms and slid round her waist, imprisoning her against him. Tara could feel the warm wetness of his soaking clothes seeping through her own, became hotly aware that her saturated slacks and top clung to her slender curves, as revealing as a dancer's leotard, then her awareness blurred and she became conscious only of Bryn, of his hard male strength pressing her against him, of his hand cupping the back of her head, tilting her face upwards the better for his lips to explore its delicate contours. A shiver ran through her as they teased along the slender line of her throat. Her heart pounded, and she felt herself go pliant in his arms, and her hands rose to clasp him round his neck.

'You passed your test with flying colours,' he murmured approvingly.

So he *had* been testing her! The patronage of it stuck in her throat, choking her. Had he tested her to see if her courage matched the task he set her? Or was it to discover if she had the courage to defy him, and refuse the task entirely? It little mattered now either way, his arrogant assertion was enough, and Tara pulled away from him as if she had been stung.

'Do I get a signed diploma from you to prove it?' she lashed out sarcastically. Her hands dropped down and pushed against his broad chest, striving to push him away from her. 'Keep your congratulations!' she stormed at him angrily. 'Offer them to Meli. She might appreciate them—I don't!'

'Come and be introduced to my son, Bryn. Meet Paul junior!' Paul came to stand at the top of the van steps with the baby in his arms, and a proud smile lighting his face.

'I'll go and see if Meli needs anything.' Hurriedly Tara grasped at her opportunity to escape.

'Meli's asleep. I thought I'd bring out the baby to show to Bryn, and then go back inside and sit with her for a while,' Paul said.

It was impossible to intrude between husband and wife. Setting aside her right to remain in her own caravanette, Tara could not bring herself to make an unwanted third in that once-in-a-lifetime private hour between a man and his wife, and their firstborn. And yet, if she did not remain in the van, where else was she to go? She hesitated irresolutely, and Paul moved aside from the doorway, his look betraying a belated attack of conscience at depriving her of her home.

'Don't let me prevent you,' he began with ill-concealed reluctance.

'You're not,' Bryn answered for her before she had time to speak, keeping his arms round her and himself preventing her from mounting the van steps. 'Tara and I were just going to stroll down to the beach to watch the sun rise,' he told Paul.

Every instinct made Tara long to shout at Bryn that he lied, that she had no intention of going to the shore, or anywhere else, with him. She longed to hurl herself out of his arms and run up the steps of the van past Paul, and repossess her own vehicle, there to fling herself on to her bunk and release the storm of tears that stung the sight from her eyes, and closed her throat, and made her incapable of denying Bryn's claim, and equally incapable of spoiling Paul's perfect hour.

'These islands are famed for their sunrises and sunets—but of course, being a courier, you'd know that.'

She did know it. She had watched the sun rise and set over the Pacific islands many times, but never before with Bryn. His presence brought a new significance to the spectacle that unfolded itself before them, a disturbing significance that flaunted itself in streamers of fire as the sun turned the lashing sea to molten gold, and wrapped the sky in trailing scarves of brilliant colour that changed with bewildering speed from pale saffron to flaming orange and angry red, matching her turbulent mood as she stood in silence beside him, watching it with mutinous eyes.

'That's the end of the show for this morning.'

The sun swung high, already warm, and the colours faded to a uniform blue, while a feeling of flatness invaded Tara, bringing the desolation back.

'Your clothes are steaming.' With a sense of unreality she watched the small vapour cloud grow about Bryn's body as the rays of the sun increased in strength. It gave her a peculiar feeling inside to watch the vapour cloud, like thin smoke surrounding him, rising from his shirt and shorts that were wet from the storm. She had thought of him as Vulcan when she first saw him, the god of fire striding towards her across the beach, scattering sand smoke in the wind as he came.

'So are yours. You'd better go back to the caravanette and change.'

'Not yet.' She leaned back against a handy rock and clasped her hands about her knees. 'Paul and Meli . . .' She stopped, and allowed her reason for not going back to hang unspoken in the air between them. Refusing to allow that there might be another, more potent reason for her reluctance to return. 'The sun will dry us off quickly enough now the storm's passed.' Not even to herself did she want to admit her real reason for not wishing to return to the caravanette, that only minutes before she had not wanted to leave.

'I might go beachcoming first.' Bryn's expression showed his doubt as to the validity of her first excuse,

so she hastily latched on to another, more selfish
reason for not returning to the van, grasping at the
first thing that caught her eye. 'The storm's left an
interesting-looking pile of flotsam and jetsam at the
edge of the tide.' A variety of birds darted in and out
of the rubbish, themselves indulging in their own form
of beachcombing, and Tara watched them lazily.
Suddenly they took fright and rose with startled cries,
flapping away to drop down again beside another pile
of sea-wrack further along the shore, and Tara sat up
interestedly, her attention caught by the reason for
their disturbance. A small four-footed creature with a
long tail darted with quick movements among the piles
of debris, searching, like the birds, for whatever it
might find.

'It's a mongoose, looking for an easy breakfast.'

'I've heard they're common on the islands, but I've
never seen one before.'

The mongoose became a bridge, spanning her
anger. Bryn leaned down and pulled her to her feet,
and his firm grasp drew her across the bridge, her feet
hesitant at first, and half afraid as he suggested
casually,

'Let's wander down and see if he's found anything.'

The sun was warm on her back, Bryn's hand was
warm round her own, and suddenly her anger
evaporated like the moisture drawn by the sun from
their clothes, and it was good to go with him to see
what it was the mongoose had found, good to share the
experience together. Tara's feet gained a new
eagerness, hastening her steps, and the startled
mongoose scuttled away, chewing at something that
dangled from its jaws. Its rejection of their company
left a brief, bleak feeling behind it, but not for long,
because the animal had rejected Bryn as well as
herself, and his amused laugh melted the bleakness
away, so that she laughed with him, and without

knowing how it happened they were two children together, exploring the new, storm-washed world of the beach.

'I wonder what it found to eat?'

'I shouldn't enquire too closely, if I were you,' Bryn advised her sagely. 'It's probably something quite unspeakable, washed up by the tide.'

The questions that teemed through Tara's mind were equally unspeakable, in quite a different way, and they all centred on Bryn. Who was he? Where did he come from? Why was he travelling alone? And others to which she dared not give thought room, because she might find the answers even more unspeakable. A ripple of unease shivered through her at what those answers might be, and the illusion of childhood vanished with the shiver. The electric impulses that sparked from Bryn's fingers through her arm, through her heart, did not belong to childhood, nor did her nervous awareness of him, tall and straight beside her, of his easy, flat-hipped stride that stretched her own much shorter legs to a trot to keep up with him.

'How did you know what to do last night, when Meli . . .?' Hastily she broke into speech, tossing one of the less loaded questions that teased her, like a ball through the air between them, mutely entreating him to toss it back to keep it going as something on which to focus her attention now the mongoose was gone, anything rather than allow the silence to flood back and become filled with those other questions she dared not ask, and the answers she dreaded to hear.

'It isn't the first newcomer I've helped into the world,' he replied easily, and she caught a painful breath. Did he mean his own children? A pang passed through her. It must be that, or else . . .

'If you've helped babies into the world before, you must be a doctor?' She voiced the second alternative, because the first was too painful to be borne, the while she fanned into flame a saving spark of anger that welled up inside her because he had not told her he was a doctor. Such a reassurance would have made all the difference to her last night. Resentment joined the anger, that he should dare to criticise her own lack of experience, and consequent fear, when to him such an occurrence was an everyday event.

'Not human babies.' So it could not be his own children. The relief made her feel weak, and ashamed of her weakness, that his answer should matter so much to her.

'Then what?' she hardly dared to ask. She scorned herself for asking, and her voice, even in her own ears, sounded stiff and stilted.

'Calves, to be precise.'

'Calves?' she echoed bewilderedly, and the anger inside her hardened as his eyes laughed down at her, blue pools of amusement that watched her step into the trap he deliberately laid in her path. 'Then you're not a doctor,' she discovered flatly, and stubbornly refused to ask him what else he might be, declining to give him the satisfaction of once more stumbling into his trap by pretending a disinterest she wished fervently was genuine.

'I'm a cowhand—sort of,' he drawled, and added, 'but I reckoned what was good for calves had to be good for human babies as well.' He did not evade her question, but neither did he answer it. His prevarication nettled Tara, and she kept her eyes on the ground, refusing to look up at him, refusing to show that his answer mattered to her. She could feel his eyes looking down on her, waiting for her reaction, boring through the top of her head like twin suns that set her thoughts on fire.

'A cowhand—with a yacht?' The fire forked her tongue, and her sarcasm said she did not believe him.

'Let's walk as far as the headland and see if the yacht's still afloat.'

He deliberately allowed the ball to drop, refusing to be drawn, and left the half answered question hovering tantalisingly in the air between them, as raw as a challenge. Dared she take it up, and risk what she might hear, or . . .? Tara felt the tension rear up inside her again, like tightly stretched elastic, threatening to snap.

'The yacht probably sank in the hurricane last night.' Her courage was not equal to the challenge, and she wished her ill wish on the yacht instead because it was Bryn's possession, wanting to punish him for the pain he was inflicting upon her by just being with her.

'It's still afloat.' Her lack of charity met the fate it deserved. 'She hasn't dragged her anchor.' He spoke as if it was a foregone conclusion that any anchor he put down would remain where he dropped it, no matter how adverse the weather conditions, and bitterly Tara wished her own personal anchor was as steady as his. She felt as if she had been cut adrift and blown off course, at the mercy of cross-currents of emotion against which she had not the strength to remain afloat.

'It's a wonder it survived the night, in seas like this,' she commented sourly. 'You should have brought it further into the shelter of the bay.' She criticised his seamanship, using argument to divert her thoughts.

'There's not enough depth in the bay itself for the *Roseanne*.'

'The boats that ply between the islands come right into the bay,' she insisted contrarily. 'The boats that served the sugar plantation came—I used their landing stage myself yesterday.' She ignored the fact that it was no longer visible under the mountainous green combers that lashed the shore, still driven by the fury of the gale just passed.

'The inshore vessels have got a shallow draft. The *Roseanne*'s an oceangoing yacht, she needs deep water.'

'It looks deep enough to me,' Tara persisted. It was easier to argue with Bryn than to allow her mind to dwell upon him.

'There's a coral reef stretching across the bay from about halfway along the headland,' he answered, brushing aside her argument. 'There's no way through the reef, and only a flat-bottomed craft could pass over it in safety, which makes it an effective barrier against the larger vessels, to the calmer waters inshore.'

There was no way through the barrier between herself and Bryn. It hovered like a tangible presence between them, with perilous fangs sharper than any coral, hiding just beneath the surface, ready to rend and destroy if she should venture to cross it, effectively leaving her at the mercy of the stormy waters on the other side. Blindly she struck out in a desperate attempt to keep herself afloat.

'Now the hurricane's passed, I'll run the van back round to the other side of the island.' She disengaged her hand from Bryn's and brushed non-existent sand particles from her slacks as she moved restlessly away from his side, striving to make her voice sound normal. The storm inside her was far from over, and being on the other side of the island, on the other side of the world for that matter, would offer no escape from her thoughts of Bryn. 'I can take Meli and the baby back to their home at the same time,' she added practically, as if that, and no other, was the overriding reason for her need to get away.

'You won't be able to leave this side of the island for a couple of days at least,' Bryn stated baldly, and Tara stared at him, outraged.

'You commandeered my van so that Meli could have her baby in comfort,' she cried angrily, 'but that doesn't mean you can keep it, now the emergency's over. I want my vehicle back, and I intend to have it. Once I've dropped Meli and the baby, I'll park on the beach where I was before. After the wind last night, there shouldn't be any coconuts left to drop off the palm trees,' she finished bitingly.

'What route do you intend to take, to get back on to the windward side of the island?' he enquired silkily. His tone should have warned her, but she was too angry to take heed, and she rushed on regardless.

'The same route I took when I first arrived on the island—along the beach, of course,' she replied shortly.

'The way the wind's still driving the water, the beaches will be covered for the next forty-eight hours, even at low tide,' he told her bluntly, and Tara stared back at him, at bay. 'Take a look, it's low tide now.' He caught her by the shoulders and turned her round to face the headland around which she had driven when she first landed. She did not want to look. She did not want to believe him. Every nerve of her cried out that it must not be true, but ruthlessly he forced her to look, obliging her to believe the evidence of her own eyes, and despair gripped her as she gazed at the great, white-tipped combers, three times their normal size, which battered the headland, drowning the only possible route open to her. There was another route. She knew it, and Bryn knew it, as he must also know that it was one she dared not attempt alone. The journey over the ancient track across the mountain was an expedition that demanded courage of a high order—Bryn's order, not her own. Her shoulders slumped under his hold, and she turned away with dragging feet to follow him back towards the caravanette.

'I'm stuck here myself,' he shrugged his acceptance of the inevitable, and a knot of misery twisted inside

Tara's stomach at the resignation in his voice, that held no pleasure at the prospect of his protracted stay, no pleasure in the prospect of her company . . .

'I can't get back to the *Roseanne* until the water's calmed down, and it usually takes a couple of days after a blow like we endured last night,' he finished philosophically.

Two days. How was she to bear it? Tara wondered bleakly. Forty-eight hours of torment, in Bryn's constant company, and with the wildly tossing yacht an agonising reminder of the one question, more vital to her than all the others, at the forefront of her troubled mind.

Who was Roseanne?

CHAPTER FOUR

'WHERE did you put the ignition key to the van, Paul?'

Bryn's voice, speaking close to her ear, sounding through the thin walls of the van, cutting through the enveloping mists of sleep. Tara blinked and opened her eyes, and heard Paul reply,

'I gave it back to Tara, after I'd parked the van here.'

'Then I'll go into the van and get it.'

'I don't know where Tara put it.' Paul sounded doubtful.

'If she'd parked the van herself, she'd have left it in the lock.' There was an unmistakable laugh in Bryn's voice, and it brought Tara wide awake, jolting her out of the refreshing slumber that made up for her loss of sleep the night before. 'She'll have left it lying around somewhere, I guess.' He sounded unflatteringly confident of her carelessness.

'She may sleep for a while yet. She was pretty tired after last night.' Paul again, and then Bryn, answering him.

'I don't need to wake her. When I've found the key I'll move the van with Tara inside it.'

'You'll move nothing!' Indignation sat Tara bolt upright on the bunk, furious to discover Bryn plotting for the second time to take possession of her caravanette. Angrily she slid her legs over the edge of the bunk, prepared to do battle to retain possession of her vehicle, and discovered the opposite bunk was empty.

'Meli?'

Meli was missing, and so was the baby. The bunk was straightened, and the covers tidied as if she had never lain there.

'Meli's lying down in the shade of the kiawe trees.' Bryn jackknifed himself through the van doorway and perched negligently on the end of her bunk, and Tara knew a moment's swift relief that she had gone to sleep just as she was, in her slacks and top, too weary to change into the freedom of her all-too-brief cotton nightie. 'Paul and I carried her there. We left you here to sleep it off.'

'You make it sound as if I was sleeping off a hangover!' She turned on him wrathfully, and wished she could blame her unco-ordinated thoughts on something so simple as alcohol. Bryn was far more potent than any cocktail, and the effect of his close proximity was more unnerving than any indulgence in wine.

'What do you want my van for this time?' she enquired sharply. 'Surely there's not another baby due?'

'Heaven forbid!' Bryn exclaimed. 'One was quite enough, under those conditions.'

'One was more than enough, so far as I was concerned,' Tara retorted unforgivingly.

'So will the heat be, if the van remains on these rocks for much longer. I'm going to move it under the shade of the trees, now the hurricane's passed. We moved Meli and the baby over an hour ago.'

'And left me to roast in the heat of the van,' Tara realised resentfully, becoming aware for the first time how stifling was the air under the metal roof. 'Thanks for nothing,' she finished bitterly.

'You were asleep,' Bryn shrugged. 'Now you're awake, I'll move the van if you'll tell me where you put the ignition key.'

If his conversation with Paul was anything to go by, he intended to move it anyway, whether she was awake or not, but Tara felt too hot to argue.

'I left the key somewhere around,' she said

carelessly, slipping off the bunk and round Bryn and heading for the door. 'I'll leave you to look for it. I'm going to talk to Paul.' She knew where she had left the key, it was hung in its usual place on a hook beside the stove, but, 'Let Bryn stay in the heat of the van and look for it,' she muttered vindictively. 'He left me there, so why shouldn't I leave him?'

'How' the baby?' she enquired aloud of Paul, and the new father grinned across at her from his task of refilling the water container at the spring.

'Six hours old, and nearly talking,' he boasted, and Tara laughed.

'I'll go and join Meli, and see for myself.' She headed in the direction of a clump of kiawe trees further along the shore, beckoned by Meli's waving hand. It looked cool and inviting under the trees, and made the lava rock on which she trod seem doubly hot. The heat penetrated through the soles of her sandals, and beat back in a white glare that was painful to her eyes.

'I wish I'd put on my sunglasses.' She hesitated for a fraction, then shrugged and continued walking. The sunglasses were in the van, but so was Bryn, and if she went back for them he might make her help him hunt for the ignition key. 'I'd rather risk a headache,' she decided, and felt the first warning throb echo in her temples as the van engine coughed into life behind her.

'He's found the key,' she diagnosed. 'He must have X-ray eyes,' she decided crossly, put out that he had not had to endure the heat in the van for more than a couple of minutes before he discovered the missing key. She paused, disconcerted, as the van engine shunted uncertainly several times before it finally began to run smoothly under Bryn's patient coaxing.

'Mind what you're doing to my van, it's got to last for the rest of my holiday,' she muttered, and watched

balefully as Bryn swung it round and began to run it
cautiously in her wake.

'Would you like a lift?' He pulled up beside her and
stuck his head out of the driving window, and Tara
hated him for his grin as he looked down on her hot
face.

'No,' she snapped, and kept on walking, hating him
still more when he took her at her word and engaged
gear and ran the van past her. The wheels churned up
a cloud of dust from the rock as he went by, and it
blew in a gritty stream in her face and hair, making
her eyes smart, and adding to her perspiring
discomfort.

'You *do* look hot.' Meli's sympathy did little for
Tara's morale, and she slumped down beside the other
girl, irritably conscious of the contrast between her
own crumpled attire, and Meli's crisp, clean sundress,
becomingly patterned in red and white, and set off
with a fresh scarlet pom-pom flower pinned in her
smoothed-back hair.

'I'm hot and dusty. The wheels of the van showered
me with grit, and most of it went in my eyes,' Tara
glowered accusingly in Bryn's direction.

'Let me look,' he responded instantly. 'It isn't wise
to allow a foreign body to remain in your eye.'

It was not wise to allow a foreign body to get under
her skin, Tara thought sharply, but this enigmatic
man had succeeded in doing just that, and it was going
to take more than the rolled-up corner of a
handkerchief to remove him, she acknowledged
helplessly.

'There's no need.' Hastily she backed away from his
outstretched hand, declining his ministrations. It was
not wise to allow him to touch her, either. In fact, it
was folly of the worst kind to get anywhere near him,
and for the next forty-eight hours she would need all
her ingenuity to avoid contact with him. 'I blinked the

grit away,' she excused herself, and complained hurriedly to Meli, before he could insist, 'I feel grubby. I'd love a dip.'

'The sea's too rough,' the other girl frowned anxiously.

'I know, I wouldn't dare venture into the combers,' Tara assured her.

'There are plenty of tide pools higher up the beach, that are perfectly safe for swimming in,' Bryn remarked offhandedly. 'Hold on, Paul, I'll help you to turn your canoe.' He broke off and strode away to join Paul on the fringe of the trees, and together the two men bent to attend to the outrigger canoe and bring it into a position where it caught the most shade, then they busied themselves in covering it with palm leaves, while Tara watched them at their task with brooding eyes.

'The wood dries out and cracks if it's left lying in the sun.' Mercifully Meli thought she was interested in what the men were doing, and not in the men themselves. Or one man, Bryn, to be precise. Hurriedly Tara averted her eyes.

'The canoe doesn't look strong enough to stay afloat,' she remarked.

'It's strong enough,' Meli replied confidently. 'Little Paul will have his first ride in it as soon as the sea calms down, and Paul's able to take us both home.' She gazed down fondly at her infant son, quietly asleep in the open wickerwork basket that made an ideal cradle in the warm temperatures of the island.

'I'll take you back in the van,' Tara protested.

'Thanks, but no, we'll go back home the way we came—together,' Meli refused smilingly, and Tara swallowed a sudden lump in her throat, shut out by the other girl's happiness.

'I'll change into my swimsuit and go and find that tide pool.' She climbed the steps of the van with feet that dragged, viewing the prospect of her solitary swim without enthusiasm. Why should a holiday on her own, that had seemed so appealing when she set out, appear so unattractive now? It was the same holiday, and she was the same person. Not quite the same person. Resolutely she closed her mind to the difference since she met Bryn. 'He's nothing but a casual acquaintance, a ship that passes in the night.' Clichés did not help either, she discovered, and divested herself of her crumpled clothes and changed into her swimsuit with hardly a glance at its up-to-the-minute emerald green smartness in which she had rejoiced when she bought it. Holidaying on her own, she had not bothered to bring a wrap with her.

'A towel will have to do.' She slung the white terry towelling crossways over her shoulder, and surveyed its skimpy length with discontented eyes. 'I wish it was a foot or so longer.' It was not that she was shy of meeting Bryn. Paul was there, too, of course, so why hadn't her thoughts included him as well? She shrugged them aside before they provided their own unwanted answer, and ran defiantly down the van steps. Perhaps Bryn was still with Paul and the canoe, and would not notice how she was dressed anyway.

'I love your swimsuit.' Meli noticed, and her black eyes took in Tara's slender figure enviously. 'Roll on the day when I can get back into mine,' she sighed.

'We'll tell you what the water's like when we come back.' Bryn eased himself upright from his leaning post against the side of the caravanette, and Tara spun round with a gasp.

'We?' Her quick movement dislodged the towel from off her shoulder, and she grabbed at its scanty cover, confused colour rushing to her cheeks as she caught the glint in Bryn's eyes that roved with unashamed approval over her slender outline.

'As if he was admiring the outlines of his yacht!' she

thought furiously, and found the thought instantly qualified with another, less welcome one, 'or its namesake, Roseanne.'

'We?' she repeated belligerently, and her dismayed eyes remarked the fact that Bryn, too, had changed, into dark red swimming trunks that the unbroken tan of the rest of his athletic frame told her were his regular attire in the heat.

'We,' he repeated mockingly, and moved towards her, taut muscles rippling smoothly in a perfectly proportioned body that carried not a single surplus ounce, she noticed bemusedly.

'You'll need a pair of shoes on your feet.' He glanced critically at her bare toes.

'I shan't need to wear shoes to walk along a sandy beach,' she objected instantly. 'He'll be telling me what make-up to wear, next,' she mutinied silently, and repeated aloud, to make sure he had got the message that she would not be dictated to, especially by him, 'I shan't . . . ooh!' It was long, and needle-sharp, and she removed it with urgent fingers, hopping on one foot with an anguished expression on her face.

'Kiawe thorns have got some pretty sharp points,' he stated unnecessarily. He did not say, 'I told you so.' He did not need to, Tara decided irately, his expression said it for him as he watched her antics with a marked lack of sympathy. 'You need something with good stout soles,' he advised gravely, and stood aside with ostentatious politeness to allow her to re-enter the caravanette.

'You . . .!' She flounced past him and stormed up the steps to grab at her sandals—then just as quickly discarded them. The sandals had neither heels nor toes, and her smarting foot cried out against possible further contact with the kiawe thorns.

'My canvas sneakers with the rope soles,' she

remembered. The soles were thick and strong, and so was the canvas that enclosed her toes, ideal for the purpose. She reached them out and laced them on, taking as much time as possible in doing it.

'Let Bryn wait for his swim,' she muttered rebelliously, and dallied in the van until she could not find an excuse to delay there any longer.

'He's gone!' She reappeared, and it was like a slap in the face to find him missing. Far from being annoyed because she had kept him waiting, he had not bothered to wait for her. She could see his back, tall and straight, disappearing towards the edge of the trees as he picked his way through a clutter of miscellaneous small craft that were now gathered together in the shade.

'Beast!' Tara hissed, illogically resenting the fact that the target of her malice had removed himself out of range. 'Beast, for not waiting for me!'

'Mmm? Did you say something?' Meli asked her drowsily.

'No, nothing of any importance,' Tara replied shortly. Bryn was of no importance to her. She must not allow him to become important.

'Not that way. Over here.'

Deliberately Tara set out in the opposite direction from Bryn, and instantly he shouted her back again.

'As if he was shouting to some disobedient puppy,' she decided crossly. 'Well, I won't come to heel. He can shout as much as he likes!' She continued walking.

'If you want to swim, the tide pool's in this direction!'

She did want to swim. More than anything else at the moment, she longed to feel cool water against her skin, laving away the trauma of the night. It was a magnet, pulling her feet irresistibly in Bryn's direction, dragging the reluctant rest of her with them.

'I thought you'd decided not to bother.' She could

not quite hide her pique because he had not waited for her, but to her chagrin he did not seem to notice her dark mood.

'I came to fetch a grass mat from my dinghy,' he answered her casually. 'This coral sand sticks to your skin like glue if you lie out to dry after a swim.' He lounged on the edge of his boat waiting for her to come up to him, and she could see the grass mat rolled up under his arm.

'You've come well prepared,' she acknowledged grudgingly. The mat looked wide enough for two people to lie upon it. Perhaps he normally shared it with Roseanne? His dinghy gleamed white, bright with new paint, its rowlocks shone silver in the sun, and a sizeable outboard motor weighted down the rear end, an alien thing among the outrigger canoes. The yacht's name, *Roseanne*, was emblazoned in neat black letters along the boat's side. Tara stared at it, and then hurriedly averted her eyes and said ungraciously,

'I've got my towel to lie on.' She could not bring herself to share the grass mat with Bryn, to lie in the place that Roseanne would normally occupy.

'When I beached, I guessed it might take a day or two before I could get back to the yacht, so I came equipped.'

He stood up lazily and shouldered the mat like a gun, cupping the end of it in the palm of one hand, while his other reached out and found Tara's fingers, and drew her with him out from under the shade of the trees and into the hot sunshine along the beach. His grip was light but firm, not too tight to be uncomfortable, but not loose enough for her to be able to slip her hand free from his without a struggle. Every instinct in Tara cried out a warning for her to wrench her hand free and fly from the electrifying contact that made the sun more brilliant, and the sky a deeper blue, as blue as the colouring of Bryn's eyes that looked down into her own, and did alarming things to her pulse rate.

But the beach was populated this morning by fisherfolk gleaning the tideline where the mongoose had sought its early meal, and in the face of their friendly greetings it was impossible to create a scene, and indulge in a struggle that she was certain to lose anyway. Tara gritted her teeth and left her hand where it lay, uneasily aware that she soon might need to cling to Bryn's hand for support. Her racing pulse left her breathless and curiously lightheaded, causing her legs to send out urgent signals that they must soon reach the tide pool and allow her to sit down, or else . . .

'There's the tide pool!' A wave of relief flooded over her as it came into view. Several small children were already playing in the shallow water, splashing each other with shouts of glee.

'That one's too shallow for us to swim in. There's another pool, further along the beach.' Bryn carried on walking, and somehow Tara forced her legs to keep pace with him, one trembling step after another until, after what seemed like a hundred miles, but could not have been more than a few yards, the gleam of another pool caught her eye.

'Thank goodness!' she gasped.

'We can't swim here, either,' Bryn dashed her surge of hope. 'There's a man fishing this pool, he won't thank us for disturbing the water.' He indicated the bronze figure skilfully casting a hand net across the pool, hunting the fish left marooned by the receding tide, employing a method as old as the island itself, and the timeless patience of a people whose heritage had taught them the value of being able to wait.

'Let's stay here and watch him for a minute or two,' Tara begged. If only she could stand still for a while, maybe Bryn would loose her hand and her pulse rate might return to normal. With uncanny accuracy her fingers seemed to read her thoughts, and they instantly tightened with a convulsive life of their own, gripping Bryn's hand as if they intended never to let it go. Tara felt them move, and a shiver of pure dismay coursed through her. If she could not control her own reflexes, how could she hope to control the impossible demands of her heart?

'I thought you wanted to swim?' His hand urged her on. 'The next pool's deeper, much better to swim in.'

It was deep, and blue, and crystal clear, with a sandy bottom and brilliantly coloured fish that darted like miniature rainbows in their crystal element. 'What more could you want?' Bryn teased her. 'Good bathing, fine beaches, and tropical sunshine. Isn't this what you came to the island to find?'

She had found all those and something more, something she had not come looking for, and the pain of the one thing more she wanted, the one unattainable thing, closed her eyes in a brief, agonised shutting out of the first three.

'I'll spread out the grass mat here. Do you want to put your towel on top of it, to keep it free from sand? Otherwise, when you come to rub yourself dry, it'll feel like an emery board.'

Tara tossed him her towel, but she did not wait to see him drop it on to the grass mat. Her eyes stung a warning, and fearful lest their unnatural brightness betray her, she turned and dived into the pool, and the sunwarmed water gave her shelter, and for the moment at least, an illusion of security. It steadied her pulse and took away the sting from her eyes, and she surfaced and rolled over on her back and floated, in control of herself again, so that she was able to call out to Bryn in a more or less normal voice,

'This is what *I* came to the island for. What about you? Apart from seeking shelter from the hurricane, I

mean?' She neatly blocked his answer that would tell
her nothing she did not already know.

'I came into the area for the fishing.'

'Fishing?' she echoed. His answer was so unexpected, it turned her upright in the water, and she
screwed up her eyes against the sun and quizzed his
face, not knowing whether to believe him or not.
'What sort of fish? These?' It seemed incredible that
he should sail a yacht all the way to the Pacific to catch
fish such as were in the tide pool, however brightly
coloured.

'Those are nothing but tiddlers,' he dismissed them
scornfully. 'I came for the real sport—the big marlin.'
He hunkered down on the rock bank and stared back
at her intently. 'The marlin are fighting fish, worthy
of the chase.'

'If you can catch them,' she taunted him recklessly.

'I catch anything I choose to chase.'

There was no mistaking his meaning. Tara gasped
and swallowed water, and choked on the raw salt taste
of it. She gurgled and spat, and hated Bryn's mocking
laugh as he rose from his crouch in one smooth
movement, swung his arms above his head, and sprang
from off the rock like a spring uncoiled, in a perfect
dive towards her. She saw his body arc through the
air, but she did not wait to see him hit the water. With
a frantic splash she turned and swam for dear life,
scooping herself through the water with panicky arms
that, after the first dozen or so strokes, screamed out
in fierce protest at the unaccustomed strain. Her chest
heaved for breath, and she tossed a glance over her
shoulder, but there was no sign of Bryn, only the
ripples made by her own mad dash across the pool.
She shook her head to clear her eyes. He must be
there, she had seen him dive, so if he was not on the
surface, then he must be . . .

'No, Bryn. No!'

He struck from beneath her, swift and silent, homing in on his quarry with a deadly accuracy that, if she had been a fish, would have meant one less marlin in the sea.

'Let go of me—I'm not a marlin. Loose me!'

Half laughing, half crying, she splashed and fought, but his strength made nonsense of her struggles. She surfaced, gasping for air, and he let her go for a second or two until she got her breath back, then his hands reached out towards her again.

'Don't you dare . . .' She splashed him. With the flat of both hands she used the only weapon at her command, and hit the surface of the water as hard as she could, sending a shower of spray straight into his face. The force of the blow stung her palms until they felt as if the skin must have split straight across, and Bryn clawed water off his face, temporarily blinded by her swift retaliation. With an eel-like wriggle Tara grabbed her opportunity and dived, using his own tactics to evade him.

'You little witch!'

His voice reached her seconds before the water closed above her head, shutting off the surface sounds, shutting her in with an unreasoning panic that must rival that of the marlin when it knew the hunt was on, and capture was only a matter of time.

He coursed her under water, a silent threat behind her, matching her desperate pace with effortless ease. He reached out a hand and touched her ankle, and she could feel the ripple of his amused laugh as she kicked frantically to free herself, and galvanised her arms and legs in a flurry of furious effort to try to outdistance him. The pool seemed as wide as the Pacific Ocean, and Tara felt her strength begin to wane, until, spent and breathless, she was forced to surface, and turned, panting, to face him.

'Nicely landed!' He scooped her up triumphantly in

his arms and floated her on the surface of the pool while he trod water above her. She could see the sky shining blue behind his head, his eyes were a blue brilliance above her face, coming closer, blotting out the sky. She strained her head back arching away from him, and the move ducked her face under water, and brought her spluttering to the surface again to meet the forceful pressure of his lips to which she must either submit, or drown. She drowned in the wild exhilaration of his kiss, lost to all sense of time and place as his lips explored her mouth, her cheeks, and moved on tantalisingly across her bare tanned shoulders.

'You're a nymph, a green sea nymph,' he murmured huskily.

'Sea nymphs have long blonde hair, to lure sailors to their doom.' She twined her fingers in his hair, feeling the strong, vital springiness of it defying the water of the pool.

'Those are mermaids, not nymphs, and anyway I'm a yachtsman, so I don't count.'

And the name of his yacht was *Roseanne*. The memory pricked like the kiawe thorn, goading Tara back to reality.

'I'll race you to the side.' Swift as the thought, she untwined her fingers from his hair and put her hands against his broad chest, and pushed. The unexpected move caught him unawares, and the push broke her free from his arms, and she was away, racing for the bank, as if by speed alone she could leave her feelings behind her as she hoped to leave Bryn. It was a forlorn hope, as she knew it must be. In seconds Bryn caught up with her, and side by side they raced for the bank. Tara exerted all her strength to keep in front of him, but she was hopelessly outclassed.

'Give me your hand.' He easily got there first, and swung himself up on to the rocks, then he reached down and pulled her out of the water to stand beside him, out of the security of the pool so that, suddenly confused, she looked away, and pretended to search for her towel.

'Where did you put it?'

'On the grass mat.' He put her there as well, lifting her with effortless hands across the intervening stretch of sand so that it should not stick to her wet feet. She had not intended to sit on the grass mat with him, and her feet cringed from the contact, but once there the urge to remain beside him was too strong, and she lost that race as well, and sat down and began to rub her hair with the towel, letting it drop over her face so that her expression should not betray her thoughts to him.

'Let me do it for you.' He took the towel from her hands and rubbed briskly, and she closed her eyes and gave herself up to the feel of his fingers massaging her head.

'The sun will do the rest.' She would much rather Bryn did it for her. She wanted to cry out to him to keep on rubbing, but he turned the towel's attention to his own hair instead.

'Let me.' She turned and reached up, eager to perform the same service for him, eager for any excuse to cradle his head in her hands, but he tossed the towel aside and leaned back lazily on his elbow, refusing her with a casual,

'I've mopped up the drips, the rest can dry by itself.'

It was like trying to gain entrance to a clam. She drew back her hands sharply, smarting from his rebuff. The moment she got anywhere near him, he shut himself into his shell with an almost audible snap.

'Suit yourself,' she shrugged. Her voice was brittle, and she was conscious of his quick, searching glance, but she deliberately avoided his eyes. If Bryn wanted to shut himself into his shell, let him, she thought vexedly. Two could play at that game, and she, Tara, did not intend to stand on the outside futilely knocking in the hope that Bryn would condescend to open up a little and let her in. She reached out and picked up the towel, and began to fold it with fingers that fumbled.

'Leave it on the mat to dry.'

'Now we've had our swim we might as well go back.' She made it sound as if there was nothing to tempt her to remain.

'Don't you want to watch the rainbows? I chose this pool because you get a good view of them from here.'

How typical of the man! Tara thought crossly. One moment he slammed the door shut in her face, and the next he opened it a tantalising crack, and invited her to peep through.

'What rainbows?' She did not want to peep, and her tone said so. 'There isn't any rain, so how can there be . . .?'

'There's one now, look. Over there,' he pointed, 'across that big outcrop of rock at the end of the bluff.'

It burst into life in a brilliant arc of colour, hung for a moment of breathless beauty, and then,

'It's gone!' Childish disappointment made her tone flat, but Bryn consoled,

'There'll be another. So long as the sun shines, and the sea remains as rough as it is now, a rainbow forms every time a big comber bursts on the rocks, and sends up a shower of spray.'

There was another, and another, just as he promised, an endless succession of transient beauty, and Tara watched the spectacle, enchanted.

'Six, seven, eight . . .' She wearied of counting the bows, and watched the rolling combers instead. 'This one will make enough spray for a bow.'

'It isn't big enough. The next one, rolling in behind it, has got a better chance.'

They made a game of it, guessing which comber would produce the best rainbow. The endless sequence of rolling water and rainbows had a curiously hypnotic effect, and watching them, Tara felt as if she was suspended in time, in a universe that consisted solely of herself and Bryn, in a paradise of sun, and sea, and rainbows.

'One more, and then we'll go back. I'm hungry.'

Prosaic, everyday needs, that intruded upon the rainbows and brought Tara back abruptly to a sense of time and place.

'Up,' Bryn urged her to her feet, 'I want to roll up the mat.'

She rose reluctantly and slipped on her rope-soled sneakers, then picked up her towel and stood aside to watch the last rainbow, this time looking at it alone because Bryn's eyes were bent upon his task of rolling up the grass mat.

A mighty comber dashed itself to destruction on the rocks, and the spray rose high and wide, and the biggest, brightest rainbow yet burst into brilliant colour over the dark bluff, but to Tara's brooding eyes the colours paled because Bryn did not share them with her, and behind the rainbow, when it faded, her eyes rested on the *Roseanne*, tossing like an uneasy thought on the troubled waters of the bay.

CHAPTER FIVE

'BARBECUED fish, salad, fresh pineapples, and avocado pears, and ... I thought you two came to Mahila to lead the simple life!' Tempting aromas drifted upwards from the glowing embers of a wood fire, and Tara surveyed the spread set out under the trees with amazed eyes.

'Come and join us,' Paul invited, 'we've prepared enough for four.'

'I don't expect you to feed me,' Tara protested, but halfheartedly. 'I've got rations in the van to last the length of my holiday.' Convenience foods, that were not half so attractive as the appetising smells now tempting her appreciative nostrils.

'Be our guest,' Meli insisted. 'You mustn't disappoint Paul by refusing his offering. He likes to show off his expertise at cookery now and again. And now and again, I encourage him,' her black eyes danced mischievously.

'This is delicious!' Tara succumbed willingly enough. 'I've never tasted fish so good before.' The light, delicate flavour was new to her, garnished with salt crystals possessing a tang that was sharp on her tongue, and made the packet salt she was familiar with seem insipid by comparison. She dipped a questioning finger and licked cautiously, the better to savour its spiciness.

'It's ocean salt,' Bryn answered her questioning look. 'The crystals are left in the tide pools when the sun evaporates the water.'

The salad, too, was strange to her palate, but crisp, and equally enjoyable, and she crunched happily.

78

'The fish was caught less than an hour ago, in one of the tide pools.' Paul looked well pleased with her obvious enjoyment. 'And the salad's actually green seaweed, gleaned from the beach this morning.' He grinned at her startled expression. 'It's good for you,' he encouraged, 'it's full of iron.'

'It tastes good, and it's appropriate to go with the fish.' Tara resolutely put aside the memory of the scavenging mongoose, gleaning its food among the seaweed, and refused to allow it to spoil her enjoyment of her gastronomic adventure.

'We passed a man using a hand net in one of the tide pools,' Bryn remembered. He sat crosslegged on the grass mat beside Tara, and ate with an enjoyment to match her own.

'The fisherman had an excellent catch, and he shared it around,' Paul answered with satisfaction. 'We've all got barbecued fish tonight,' he waved a hand to include the families of fisherfolk who were scattered in groups along the beach, eating a similar evening repast to their own, each group round its own wood fire, bright with the fuel gathered from the trees that sheltered the canoes from the sun.

'The fish in the tide pool were beautifully coloured,' Tara remembered wistfully, regarding the contents of her plate with suddenly diminished appetite.

'So is a pineapple beautifully coloured, but you don't hesitate to eat it,' Paul retorted practically. 'Have some more,' he urged her. 'Try some *poi*.'

'I mustn't eat your stores, you'll have none left for when you go home,' Tara protested guiltily.

'There are plenty more at home where these came from,' Meli assured her. 'If you help us eat our supplies, it'll save us from having to take them back when the sea calms down, and we go home tomorrow. When the sugar plantation people packed up and left the island, they leased their staff bungalows to the local fisherfolk, and to us,' she explained. 'Each bungalow had got a good patch of land already in cultivation. We grow taro roots—those are what makes the *poi*—and pineapples, and mangoes, and avocado pears. The sugar company grew its own plantations of oranges and bananas and coffee, as well as sugar cane, and although the plantations have grown wild now through neglect, the fruit's still there for the picking, as much as we want.'

The *poi* was sticky, and starchy, but pleasant enough to eat, and the avocado pears were yellow and sweet. 'Definitely not the food for slimmers,' Meli laughed.

'Tara doesn't have to worry on that score,' Bryn teased, and Tara looked up and met his laughing glance, and quickly looked away again, confused by the expression in his eyes. She turned away to hide the warm tide that flooded over her throat and cheeks, reaching for one of the small, rusty-skinned oranges piled nearby, and began to peel it with a fierce concentration, and fingers that felt suddenly nerveless and unable to retain their grip. The orange slipped and rolled, Tara grabbed at it and missed, and Bryn fielded it for her with a quick hand.

'Allow me,' he laughed at her ineffectual efforts, and dexterously finished stripping off the peel for her.

'I wonder if it's sweet?' He held out the denuded orange, and she gave it a wary look, making no attempt to take it from him.

'Try it and see.' He separated a segment to tempt her.

'You try it first.' She held back uncertainly, more nervous of contact with Bryn's hand than she was that the orange might prove to be sour.

'Coward!' He gripped the segment in his own teeth, strong and white and uncaring whether it was sweet or sour, and screwed up his face as he chewed, laughing out loud at the expression on Tara's. 'It isn't sour,' he assured her.

'You screwed up your face, so it must be.'

'I was only teasing. It's your turn now.' His laughing eyes dared her to take him at his word and bite into the segment in his fingers, taunting her because he had eaten one, and she still hesitated. 'Go on, bite it. It won't bite back.' He wedged the segment between her teeth. Briefly she felt his fingertips against her lips, warm and firm, then he cupped his hand under her chin and closed her jaws, and demanded, 'Now bite.'

She bit, and juice gushed out of the segment and over her tongue, sweet-sharp juice that curled up her taste buds and screwed up her face in a fair imitation of Bryn's own expression—not unlike the relationship between them, she thought with a flash of bitterness, with its underlying sharpness, and the ever-present threat that it might bite back if she ventured too close.

'Have some more.' He fed her the orange segment by segment, taking an occasional one for himself, then they lay back together on the grass mat and chewed contentedly until it was all gone.

'Have another orange. I've eaten nearly half of yours.'

'No, not another.' Another would not be the same. It might be sharper, and spoil the first, and Tara felt unaccountably reluctant to let anything spoil the one they had shared together.

'Coffee?' Paul strolled across and brought two steaming, aromatic cups. 'This is grown on the island, too.'

It was nectar, and Tara sipped, and relaxed under the spell of the food, and the evening, and of Bryn still stretched out beside her, drinking his own coffee, allowing it to lull her into a warm, safe cocoon that pushed the world aside and made all the tormenting, unanswered questions seem suddenly unimportant, so that when he suggested,

'Let's go and watch the sunset,' she rose eagerly.

'You'll need a wrap of some kind,' Meli warned her, 'it drops chilly after dark.'

Tara had changed from her swimsuit into a full gathered, scarlet cotton skirt and a white sleeveless top, and she chose a vididly patterned silk square, and knotted it gypsy fashion across her shoulders for extra warmth, then joined Bryn at the bottom of the van steps, conscious that her choice suited her own dark colouring. Acutely conscious of Bryn's eyes resting upon her, but he made no comment on her appearance beyond,

'You need a flower to set it off.'

'You spilled my vase of frangipani blossoms when you drove the van over the mountain.' She mourned her lost blossoms, still unable to forgive him for their destruction.

'I'll pick some more for you.'

'There aren't any frangipanis on this side of the island,' she argued, contrarily determined to load him with guilt for what he had done.

'There are plenty of ohia trees,' he dismissed the frangipanis. 'Meli's got some of the flowers in her hair. They're just the right colour to go with your skirt.'

Was there a touch of the artist in Bryn, that he saw the resemblance in the shades? Few men would have noticed. Another question, Tara thought helplessly. Another mystery to add its quota to the growing list, that must remain for ever unresolved.

'Let's go and pick one before it gets dark.' He linked his hand with hers and took her with him across the uneven surface of the ancient lava flow, and she leaned against the rough grey bark of the ohia tree and watched as he reached overhead to the bright red pompom blossoms, surreptitiously thrilling to his lean height as he stretched on tiptoe to pluck the one he wanted. 'We'll find a sprig of fern to go with it.' He found some growing in a rift of the mountain, dainty maidenhair fern that grew lush and green on the cool dank sides of the deep cleft.

'I haven't got a pin.' The buttonhole was sweet, and fresh, and lovely, and Tara yearned to wear it, but the means defeated her. 'Why didn't I bring a pin or a brooch or something with me?' She could have wept for her lack of forethought.

'Tie it in the knot of your scarf.' With sure fingers Bryn loosed the knot and slipped the flower in the silken folds of the scarf, then retied it, slightly to one side so that the flower rested just above her heart. Had he placed it there by accident or design? Her heart raced until it seemed as if he must see the flower rise and fall to the wild, swift beat of it, and she raised seeking eyes to his face, that widened to find it hovering close above hers.

'The knot's tight enough to hold the flower safely without crushing it.'

The flower stood in more danger from Bryn than from the knot. His arms clasped tightly round her, drawing her to him, and heedless of the shrinking blossom he lifted her up to meet his lips.

'Mind my flower . . .'

It was an inarticulate murmur, drugged into silence by the demands of his kiss. Between them, the gay scarlet petals of the ohia blossom lay darkened and bruised, crushed by the ardour of his embrace. Above them, unheeded, the sky flaunted an artist's palette of colour as the sunset they had come to see, set the sky on fire. Behind them, the riding lights of the *Roseanne* rose and fell restlessly on the darkening waters. Tara closed her mind to all that the lights implied, and the outside world receded, and her own world shrank until it encompassed only herself and Bryn, and the swift flaring passion between them that sent the blood leaping through her veins like a bright flame, which burned with a fierce pain that threatened to consume her, until with a long sigh she surrendered to the masterful pressure of his arms.

'La-a-a-h!'

The cry intruded from the outside world, thin, insistent, demanding to be heard, penetrating the rosy haze of her own private wonderland that needed neither flowers nor sunsets to make its joy complete. Tara stirred in Bryn's arms.

'Baby Paul wants his supper.' His voice was light and amused, and Tara felt a warm surge of gratitude to the baby for his timely warning that she must not return to the caravanette yet.

'We'll walk the long way back.' Evidently Bryn had received the message as well, and a thrill ran through her as his arm curled round her waist and turned her to walk beside him, and together they strolled across the uneven surface of the lava flow, where fissures and rocks abounded to catch at unwary feet in the swift fading light. Tara caught her toe and tripped, and he lifted her back on to her feet and suggested,

'Let's make our way back to the beach, it's smoother walking there.'

No walk with Bryn could possibly be smooth. Each minute spent in his company was beset with worse pitfalls than anything the lava flow could produce, made more hazardous by the unanswered questions that, try as she might, Tara could not obliterate from her mind.

Who was Bryn? What was he? His description of himself as 'a sort of cowhand' she dismissed out of hand. His voice and bearing alone made a nonsense out of that. So the questions remained to torment her, along with two more, even more heart-searching than the rest.

Was he married or single? And if the latter, who was Roseanne?

The lava rock gave way to sand, warm still beneath their feet from the day's sun, and pale under the rising moon. Bryn was silent, and Tara felt no inclination to talk, fearful that words might break the brittle bond between them and allow the torment of doubt and uncertainty to flow over her like the lava of old, and destroy the breathless beauty of the night that drew round them, and made them a part of itself.

Baby Paul had ceased his crying, and silence enfolded them until only the rolling combers seemed alive, and even their sullen roar, and the hissing drag of the water clawing at the edge of the beach became a part of the silence. The Southern Cross hung like a jewel in the sky, and the heaving waters borrowed a luminous beauty from the moon. They paused together by common consent at the edge of the tide, and it seemed the most natural thing in the world for Tara to turn in the circle of Bryn's arm and raise her face in mute invitation to his.

It was an invitation few men would refuse, and Bryn was not of their number. With hard arms he pulled her round to face him and bent his head above her, and his mouth accepted the invitation of her lips and plundered their soft sweetness until they felt parched by the passionate intensity of his kiss. Only Bryn knew whether or not he tasted of forbidden sweetness, and, dazzled by the pale witchery of the moonlight, for the moment Tara neither knew nor cared.

'Tara . . .' Her name came husky on his breath.

'I love you.' Her whisper mingled with her name, and both melted into the surrounding silence, and Tara closed her eyes and let her lips speak for her, and long moments of rapture passed before Bryn spoke again.

'I guess it's safe for us to go back now,' he drawled.

'Another few minutes,' Tara begged. There would never be another tropic night, another moon, another beach, to equal this. There would never be ... Her throat tightened at the negative emptiness of what would never be, and she turned her face against his shoulder lest the moisture of her eyes should reflect the moonlight, like the shine of the sea, and betray her distress to Bryn.

'I don't need to wait any longer. I've found what I came for.'

He had found her love. Tara felt as if her heart would burst with joy because Bryn had brought her here to the moonlit shore to declare his love, and in the response of her eager lips he had found what he sought, and made the treasure his own.

'Bryn ...' She murmured his name, her voice a caress.

'Now I know the *Roseanne*'s still riding her anchor without mishap, we might as well go back,' he said carelessly.

The *Roseanne*. The name was like a slap in the face. Tara jerked away from him, and the colour drained from her cheeks, leaving them a ghastly white, and her eyes wide, stricken pools in her colourless face.

'The *Roseanne*?' she echoed stupidly. 'You came to check on the *Roseanne*?'

'What else?' he shrugged, and at his words the silver melted from the moonlight, and something inside Tara seemed to snap.

'I thought ... you said ...' She stammered to a halt. He had *not* said, in so many words, that he loved her. *She* had said she loved him. In a reckless, unguarded moment of naïve trust, she had bared her heart to him, and the humiliation of it stung like a whip, belabouring her for her folly.

'How could I be such a fool?' she moaned bitterly. Her pride cringed at the memory of the way in which she had voiced her feelings, when all Bryn wanted was a light flirtation to pass the time while he checked on the *Roseanne*. He had not walked her away from the lava flow and on to the smoother beach out of concern for her comfort, but because he wanted to come down to the tide's edge to look at his yacht. Doubtless if the baby had not cried a warning to prevent them from returning to the caravanette, he would have taken her back there and gone on his own to satisfy himself that his precious vessel was still afloat. But since they could not return to the van immediately, he had amused himself with her kisses to while away the time, used her heart as a plaything, she realised bitterly, and left it broken and discarded when the game was over.

'I hate you!' Her eyes were wild in the moonlight, her breath a sharp pant that did nothing to relieve the distress of her heaving breast. 'I'll never forgive you for this—never!'

'Tara . . ' He reached out a hand to detain her, but she ducked under his arm and twisted herself free, and fled like a deer for the shelter of the kiawe trees. Their gnarled outlines stood out darkly against the pale beach, their black trunks blacker than the night, but none so black as her hatred of Bryn. Her breath sobbed in her throat as she ran, and the soft sand caught at her feet, causing her to stumble. She regained her balance and ran on, embracing the chequered darkness of the trees as a sanctuary, to hide her from his sight. The white paintwork of his boat shone faintly in the darkness, and Tara spun to avoid it and struck her shin on one of the outrigger canoes lined up ready to put to sea in the morning. The pain halted her in her tracks and she doubled up, nursing her injured member.

'Goodnight, Tara.'

Paul must have seen her coming. He strolled down the steps of the caravanette, tactfully leaving her access to her own mobile home, and she forced her hands away from the hurt on her leg and put them up

instead to brush away the tears of an even worse hurt,
that wet her cheeks like sea spray, and would
undoubtedly draw comment from Meli if she did not
manage to dry them before she entered the van.

'Goodnight, Paul.'

She forced her voice to answer, and the small
normal encounter gave her confidence to run up the
steps of the van and greet Meli lying on her bunk
inside, with a brittle cheerfulness that she hoped
would deceive the other girl, if it did not deceive
herself.

'Did you get your flower?' Meli asked interestedly.

'Yes.' Tara did not enlarge. She could not. The
unexpected mention of the flower threatened her new-
found self-control and brought a lump to her throat
that denied her utterance, and she turned hurriedly
and pulled the bud from the knot in her scarf. The
delicate stem felt hateful to her touch, a symbol of
Bryn's hypocrisy, and she longed to fling it out of the
van door, preferably at Bryn himself, whose firm step
outside made her heart race and her fingers tremble,
so that they dropped the flower on the floor and she
had to stoop to pick it up.

'I've put mine in water,' Meli's voice reached her
from the bunk. 'I left a vase ready filled for yours, it's
on the sink.

'Thanks.'

Tara did not want to keep the flower, she wanted no
reminder of her walk with Bryn, but Meli left her no
choice, so she dumped the bud in the vase and swilled
her hands to rid them of its odious touch.

'I'm glad it's not this time last night,' Meli mused,
'I wouldn't want to face that storm again.'

'If it blows again tonight I shan't hear it,' Tara lied,
and yawned widely. Meli wanted to talk, and she did
not. Her mind felt like a whirlpool, and her chances of
sleep were nil, and the last thing she felt inclined for

was an exchange of girlish confidences with the occupant of the opposite bunk.

'Goodnight, Meli.' Callously she put an end to the conversation. Her feelings were in turmoil, and she needed to be left alone to come to terms with them before tomorrow morning, a few short hours of darkness in which to face the even darker prospect of loving Bryn, and knowing he did not love her in return. Tomorrow she would have to face him again, and she would need all her courage to feign indifference. Mercifully it would not be for long.

'I'll make sure we're not left alone together again,' she vowed into the darkness. By morning the sea would be calm enough for the boats to be launched. Meli and Paul and the baby would take their canoe and go home. 'As soon as they've quit the van I'll start it up and drive back round to the windward side of the island,' she planned. She would not wait to see Bryn set off to join the *Roseanne*. 'Let him go back to his marlin fishing—I won't be used as sport for him to catch and then throw back into the sea when he's tired of the thrill of the chase!'

Her independent resolution comforted her, and she dropped into an uneasy sleep, made the more restless by a shadowy figure that hovered in the background of her dreams, refusing to be identified, and yet whom Tara was convinced must be Roseanne. And all the time Bryn's voice talked somewhere in the darkness, indistinct, so that she could not hear what it said. She strained her ears and it became gradually clearer, sounding from somewhere close to her, talking, not to Roseanne, but to Paul. Tara's eyes flew open, and discovered it was daylight, and Bryn's voice said clearly,

'I don't like the look of it, Paul. What do you make of it?'

Bryn, actually asking somebody else for their

opinion! 'I don't believe it!' Tara exclaimed aloud, and sat up rubbing her eyes.

'Neither do we. Come outside and have a look.' Meli's voice joined in, and the underlying fear in it catapulted Tara out of bed and into her skirt and top at record speed.

'What's the matter? Is it the baby?' She took the van steps at a jump, and hurried to where Meli sat on the rocks with the baby in her arms, with Paul and Bryn beside her. In her anxiety for the baby, Tara forgot her trepidation at meeting Bryn again.

'The baby's fine,' Meli responded. 'It's the sea.'

'The sea should be calm by now,' Tara frowned. She turned and stared out at the water, and her eyes widened in awe. 'It looks as if it's boiling,' she gasped. 'Just look at the yacht, it's popping up and down like a cork!' She burst out laughing at the incongruous sight of the enormous vessel bobbing up and down as if it was nothing more than a toy, then she turned and looked at Bryn's face, and the laughter died, and fear such as she had never known knifed through her. He was gazing out to sea, his eyes narrowed, looking not at his yacht as Tara expected, but out across the bay at the water itself.

'I don't like the look of it, Paul,' he repeated gravely. 'I think we'd best put the girls into the van and drive it as far up the mountain slope as we can.'

'What on earth for?' demanded Tara furiously. 'First you hijack my vehicle and bring it on to the opposite side of the island from where I want to be, and now you say you want to drive it half way back up the mountainside again!'

'Because of what's happening to the sea,' Bryn retorted harshly. 'We're in an area of volcanic activity, and tidal waves are not unknown.'

'You're talking nonsense,' Tara denounced him furiously. 'You're deliberately trying to frighten us!' If this was Bryn's way of retaliating for last night, it was a mean, underhand thing to do, to frighten Meli as well. 'If he thinks he's going to frighten me by such tactics, I'll just show him he hasn't succeeded,' she determined resolutely.

'All you're troubled about is your precious yacht,' she said aloud, scornfully. 'Stand and watch it if you want to, I'm going to get some breakfast.' She demonstrated quite clearly that his behaviour of last night had in no way affected her appetite.

'Bryn could be right, Tara,' Paul intervened in a troubled voice. 'From the look of the fisherfolk, they're thinking along the same lines,' he nodded to the group of villagers who stood deep in discussion at the edge of the trees.

'Get them all together and bring them with us as far up the mountainside as possible,' Bryn instructed him briskly.

'If it's an eruption you're worried about,' Tara argued, 'the side of the mountain is the last place to be. The tracks of the old lava flows all run down the slopes on this side.'

'The volcano's extinct,' Paul reassured her, 'it has been for a hundred years.'

'It's not the crater up there that concerns me,' Bryn sent it an indifferent glance, 'volcanic eruptions occur on the sea-bed as well as on the land, and when they do the result is. . . .'

'A tidal wave,' Paul exclaimed, and brought the conversation round full circle.

'If my reading of the sea is correct,' Bryn gave a grim nod towards the wildly disturbed water of the bay, 'there's no time to lose. Go and collect the villagers, Paul—you speak their language, I don't. I'll get the van started while you're away, and wait for you here. Get inside, Meli,' he helped her up the steps, then turned to Tara. 'You too, Tara.' His tone

towards her was peremptory, and Tara's independent
spirit rebelled.

'You don't *know* there'll be a tidal wave, you're only
guessing,' she stood her ground defiantly.

'I don't intend to wait to find out,' Bryn retorted
harshly. In one swift step he was stood over her, and
with hard hands he grasped her and swung her
straight off her feet. 'Get inside the van, and stay
there!' For the second time in their brief acquaintance
he dumped her bodily into her own caravanette, and
with a speed that left her speechless he reached out
and grabbed the ignition key off its hook beside the
stove and before she could regain enough breath to
fire the angry words that tumbled like arrows to the
tip of her tongue, he was out of the van again and
running round to the driving seat. The vehicle rocked
with the speed of his entry, and seconds later the
engine burst into life, coughed, spluttered, and died
away again.

'It did that when he started it up yesterday,' Tara
remembered with a frown.

The engine fired again, and again, briefly, and with
the same negative result, and above the sounds of
mechanical distress the agitated chattering of the
villagers reached the van and passed it as they fled in a
body towards the mountain slope, and then another
sound, sinister and far away, but growing stronger,
coming nearer, a threatening, roaring sound like a
hundred huge combers rolled into one, assailed Tara's
frightened ears.

'The engine's dead. Get out quickly, and make for
the hillside.' Bryn's face appeared at the van doorway.
'Hurry,' he urged them, 'there isn't much time!'

'Paul?' Meli hurried, and Paul came and took the
baby from her arms and lifted her down the steps.

'You support Meli on the one side, Paul, and I'll
help her on the other.' Bryn wound one strong arm

round the young mother's waist, and grasped Tara with the other.

'My skirt's caught on the van door.' She tugged at the trapped cloth with panic-stricken fingers.

'Give it to me.' Bryn took the material in a strong grip and gave it a mighty wrench. The scarlet cotton tore with a harsh ripping sound, and she was free, then Bryn's arm went round her, pressing her forward, and his voice in her ear shouted above the growing roar that rose to terrifying proportions from the bay behind them.

'Run, Tara! Run for your life . . . !'

CHAPTER SIX

TARA ran. Her heart pounded in her chest, and her breath wheezed in her throat, and she staggered up, up, forcing her failing legs up the steep sloping side of the mountain that in normal circumstances would have taxed her strength at a slow walking pace. A red mist danced before her eyes, and she stumbled and would have fallen, but Bryn's hand grasped the fullness of her skirt at the back and pulled her on to her feet again, and pressed her forward.

'I can't go any further.' Her voice came out as a hoarse croak.

'Keep going. *Run!*' Bryn's arm was a rod of steel against her back, forcing her onwards, upwards. His voice was a torment, shouting orders she had not the strength to obey. The roar behind her filled her ears like the cry of a hungry beast, racing after its prey. If only it would devour her and be done, then she could rest . . . .

'We're out of reach of the water now.'

A lifetime of agony later, Bryn's arm released her, and without its support Tara sank to her knees on the ground, utterly spent. Her eyes closed, and over the roar of the tidal wave she could hear the harsh rasp of her own tortured breath, counting the pain-filled seconds, in—out, in—out, as she opened her mouth as wide as it would go and gulped great draughts of air into her heaving lungs. Minutes passed, and hands reached down and grasped her under her armpits.

'No,' she moaned weakly. 'Leave me alone, I can't climb any further.'

'There's no need to, we're safe enough here.' Bryn's

voice penetrated the mist, calmly practical. His hands grasped and lifted her, ignoring her protests, until she was sat upright, then they pressed her backwards until she was leaning against something that felt warm and firm, something that felt gloriously safe. She opened her eyes and looked up.

'Lean back against me,' Bryn sat down beside her and drew her into the circle of his arm, resting her head back against his shoulder.

'I can't bear to look.' Meli sat with Paul and the baby close by. 'Oh, Tara, your van. . . .'

'Better the van than us,' Bryn retorted. How easily he said it! Carelessly, as if it was of no account. It did not matter, to him, Tara thought furiously, and a wave of anger as forceful as the tidal wave below them pushed aside her exhaustion, and jerked her upright out of the shelter of Bryn's arm.

'It's easy for you to say that,' she stormed, 'it isn't your van. It would be different if it was your yacht, I suppose?' What if the hire company made her pay for a replacement caravanette? The thought made her blanch. How much did such vehicles cost? She had not the vaguest notion, any more than she had of the extent of her responsibility for the safety of the hired vehicle while it was in her care. When she hired the van she signed a form, but hardly glanced at the various clauses in small print above her signature. Bitterly now she regretted her carelessness, but now was too late, and the consequences could be financially ruinous.

She stared in horror as a wall of water as high as a block of flats thundered across the entire width of the bay, racing shorewards with the speed of an express train. The sheer, awful height of it cut off the sunlight and turned the sky dark, and the whole world became a huge grey-green wave of water. The bay itself disappeared behind the white, wind-flung foam of its crest, which curled over like enormous frothing fangs. An uncontrollable shudder shook Tara from head to toe, and as if from another life she heard Paul say,

'Nothing on the beach can survive that.'

Briefly Tara remembered the mongoose, had time to hope that it had somehow managed to scuttle to safety, and then she forgot the mongoose as the tip of the wave reached the kiawe trees and roared over the canoes, over Bryn's boat. She could see the bright white paint of it gleam momentarily against the dark water as the wave caught it and tossed it high, like a plaything, higher than the trees, then engulfed it and them, along with the canoes. She longed to close her eyes as the boats disappeared into its maw, but they riveted themselves on the caravanette, and in a scene that reminded her of a slow-motion film, but in reality could only have taken a matter of seconds, she watched with stunned disbelief as the same fate overtook her mobile home.

For a few seconds the van remained in sight, pushed by the water as if it was no heavier than a toy, rolling over and over towards the mountain as if it, too, was trying to run up the slope to safety. It lost the race and began to float upside down, with its wheels sticking up in a ridiculous caricature, drifting back towards the bay as the undertow caught it and dragged it away, taking with it her clothes and her food supply, to say nothing of her passport and papers, and money. And the ohia flower which, all of a sudden, became more precious than anything else, and something she could not bear to lose. The sight proved too much for Tara's overwrought nerves, and she leapt impulsively to her feet and began to run down the slope towards the van.

'You little fool, come back!' Bryn's voice roared behind her, louder and more threatening than the waters, but Tara was beyond hearing him, beyond caring. It was easy going downhill, and she sped on with flying feet.

Mills & Boon

Love, romance, intrigue...
all are captured for you
by Mills & Boon's top-selling authors.

Take one exciting book FREE every month

Also FREE – a fashionable canvas bag.
see over for details

A sensational offer to readers of Mills & Boon, the world's largest publisher of romantic fiction.

Receive six marvellous romances each month – but only pay for five.

Yes, it's true. Accept this offer, subscribe to Mills & Boon for just six months, and you will receive one of the latest, brand new titles each month, absolutely **free!**

And you can enjoy many other advantages.

FREE BAG

Our exclusive white canvas tote bag with the Mills & Boon symbol – yours FREE – whatever you decide!

- **POSTAGE & PACKING FREE** – unlike other book clubs, we pay all the extras.
- **FREE MONTHLY NEWSLETTER** – keeps you up to date with all the new books plus offers you the chance to save even more money with special bargain book offers.
- **HELPFUL FRIENDLY SERVICE** – from the girls at Mills & Boon. You can ring them anytime on 01-684 2141.
- **THE NEWEST ROMANCES** – all six books in your monthly parcel (including the Free title) are the very latest titles which are reserved for you at the printers and delivered to you hot off the press by Mills & Boon.

10 DAY FREE TRIAL

It's so easy! Send no money now – you don't even need a stamp. Just fill in and detach the reply card and send it off today.

Should you change your mind about subscribing, simply return your first six books to us within 10 days and you will owe nothing. The tote bag is yours to keep – whatever you decide. Mills & Boon Reader Service, P.O. Box 236, Thornton Road, Croydon, Surrey. CR9 3RP

'Come back, there's nothing you can do to save the van!'

Bryn's footsteps pounded the slope behind her, running faster than her own, carrying him past her. Immediately he was a short distance in front of her he spun round to face her, and unable to stop herself on the steep slope, Tara ran full tilt into his arms.

'Let me go,' she sobbed, and with flailing hands she fought to free herself from his grasp.

'Calm down!' His hands came up and fielded her fists, then clamped on her arms above the elbows, and he shook her roughly into gasping stillness. 'Calm down!' he commanded angrily. 'It's a vehicle down there, not a human being. It isn't worth risking your life for.'

'I hired it. I'm responsible for it.' With her arms immobilised, Tara fought back with the only weapon she had left, her tongue. 'It's your fault, for bringing me to this side of the island!' she shouted at him hysterically. 'If you hadn't dragged me here, it wouldn't have happened. The tidal wave's on this side of the island, the other side would have been free, and the van would have been safe. I'll hold you responsible for its loss. I'll make you pay for it if I have to take you to court to do it!' she threatened.

'The other side of the island wasn't free of the hurricane,' Bryn shouted back at her harshly.

'What's a hurricane, compared to this?' Tara's waving hand encompassed the savage waters, and dismissed the hundred-mile-an-hour winds as a mere bagatelle.

'If we don't get back up the slope we'll be drawn into the water ourselves.' Bryn dragged her back along the way she had come, his strength making nonsense of her puny efforts to resist him. The wave raced on, and flung itself at the mountain with a challenging roar, and Tara's resistance vanished as the water leapt upwards towards them, reaching out to grasp at them, its momentum sustained by a barrage of high-speed waves racing in from the bay behind the first one. The water rushed upwards, so close that it flung wet fingers of spray in her face and hair, and she cringed against Bryn, but in the battle of the mighty, the mountain won, and with a growl of frustration the water conceded defeat and rolled backwards down the slope, and Bryn dropped Tara unceremoniously beside Meli and the baby with a curt,

'Stay with Meli and don't move, while Paul and I have a word with the fishermen and decide what best to do.'

'I'll do my own deciding,' Tara asserted independently. 'In any case, there's only one thing I can do, and that's to remain here. Thanks to you I've lost the roof over my head,' she reminded him unforgivingly. 'All the canoes are smashed to matchwood, along with your boat.' It gave her some satisfaction to know that Bryn had not come out of the débâcle completely unscathed. 'The scrub that grows on this side of the island wouldn't provide enough wood to make a raft, let alone another canoe, so until the water recedes from the beach sufficiently for them to walk back to the windward side of the island, Paul and Meli and the fisherfolk are trapped on this peninsula along with me. Unless, that is, you expect them to climb over the mountain across the track by which you dragged me here?' she asked him sarcastically. 'At least you've still got your yacht. If you can manage to reach it, that is,' she added maliciously.

'You'll need to be a strong swimmer to be able to reach it, now you've lost your boat,' Paul observed, and Meli said,

'Not all that strong,' in a peculiar voice that turned three pairs of eyes questioningly in her direction. 'The spray's died down a bit,' she explained, 'and I've just caught a glimpse of the yacht, and it looks a lot closer to the shore than I remember.'

They all turned in silence and looked seawards, registering the truth of what Meli said. Showers of white spume still blotted out the bay, but now and then it cleared for a few seconds, and in one of the intervals before the next wave obliterated their view, they saw the *Roseanne* clearly, as Meli said, close enough to the shore to be well within the reach of a strong swimmer, as Tara knew Bryn to be.

'The anchor must have dragged when the tidal wave came in,' Paul reckoned. 'It's lucky the anchor checked the yacht again before it was lifted right inshore, and beached.'

'It's effectively beached now,' Bryn answered in a clipped voice. 'It isn't the anchor that's stopped the *Roseanne*, it's the coral reef. Look at the angle of her, she isn't riding the water, she's jammed tight on something below the surface, and it's my guess she's probably holed as well.'

'Oh, Bryn!' Meli mourned, 'your lovely yacht . . .'

'Better the yacht than us,' unrepentantly Tara threw Bryn's own words back at him. Now he would have the yacht to pay for, as well as her van. She had no feelings about the loss of his vessel. She could not bring herself to regret the loss of a yacht named *Roseanne*. She felt Bryn's eyes lance through the air between them, piercing the hard outer shell of her indifference, and she stiffened defensively. If he continued to look at her like that, the shell would dissolve, and leave her vulnerable heart crying out at his loss, as it already cried out at her own, not at the loss of her van, but at the loss of her precious ohia flower. With fingers that suddenly trembled she bent and smoothed down the scarlet cotton of her skirt, then turned to Meli with a plaintive,

'I suppse you haven't got a spare pin with you? Bryn tore my skirt nearly in half when he pulled it free from the van door.' She scowled downwards at the enormous rent in the side of her skirt, almost grateful for its presence that gave her an excuse not to look up at Bryn, blaming him illogically for using unnecessary force to free her. 'Now the van's gone, I haven't got a stitch to wear except what I stand up in,' she realised with growing dismay.

'The only pin I've got is in the baby's nappy,' Meli shook her head, 'but as soon as the beaches are clear of water, and we can get back home to the other side of the island, I'll lend you some of my clothes. They'll tide you over, and you can stay with us in our bungalow for the rest of your holiday.'

'Food is a more immediate problem than clothes,' Bryn dismissed Tara's concern for her skirt as trivial, and her lips tightened ominously, but before they could frame an answer he went on, 'water, too.' He frowned and turned to Paul. 'Do you know of another fresh water spring on this side of the island, Paul? The one on the beach below us is under about six feet of sea water.'

'There isn't another one,' Paul answered in a grave voice.

'But it may be hours before the water recedes from the beach,' Meli exclaimed worriedly. 'We must have something to drink in the meantime. What about the baby?' Her lovely eyes were wide with concern as the implications of Bryn's question dawned upon her.

'If we were on the other side of the island, there'd be plenty of food growing wild, and drink as well,' Tara butted in with asperity. 'Even the milk from a coconut would be better than going thirsty.'

'There aren't any coconut palms on this side of the island,' Bryn retorted dismissively.

'I know that,' Tara snapped. 'This side of the island seems devoid of any useful form of vegetation.' She gave a disparaging glance at the surrounding scrub. 'Masses of cactus plants, and loads of berries on the scrub, aren't going to be a lot of help to us if we're marooned here for the next forty-eight hours. We don't even know whether the berries are poisonous or not.' Bitterly she regretted her non-breakfast.

'The berries are too bitter to eat,' Paul warned her. 'All' you're likely to get from them is a severe tummyache. The only thing to do is to wait until the water recedes,' he shrugged philosophically.

'We can't wait here indefinitely without food or water,' Tara responded to this piece of typical Hawaianism with scant patience. 'I'm hungry,' she complained, and glowered across at Bryn, placing the blame for her hollow state squarely on his shoulders.

'It's fashionable to be slim,' he retorted callously, and Tara gasped. Only last night he had said she did not need to slim. Only last night ... She swallowed convulsively, and the swallow cost her the opportunity to hurl a blistering retort back at him. Before she could speak, Bryn turned to Paul and said, à propos of nothing,

'Do any of the fishermen speak English, Paul?'

'Yes, the man you saw fishing with the hand net yesterday, he speaks passable English. He's got his net with him now, look, he's the one sitting on the far rock over there,' Paul pointed. 'He was repairing the net when I went to warn them of the danger this morning.' The fisherman was repairing it now. With typical Hawaiian patience he squatted on the hillside facing his vanished fishing pools, and continued his task as if it had not been interrupted.

'I'll go over and talk to him before I reconnoitre our position. Will you stay here with Meli and Tara, Paul? I don't expect to be away for very long.' Bryn scarcely waited for Paul's nod of assent before he strode off, and Tara glared at his retreating back.

'Take as long as you like!' she threw after it waspishly, but if the barb found its mark Bryn gave no response, and Tara sat on the rocks and curled her arms round her knees, hugging them to her in a vain attempt to subdue the plaintive cries from inside her that grew more insistent with each passing minute.

Bryn was away for an hour—sixty minutes of taut insecurity that not even the presence of Paul and the fishermen could alleviate.

'I don't care whether he's here or gone,' she lied robustly, but in spite of herself her eyes anxiously scanned the slopes above her, unable to tear themselves away from the track up which Bryn had disappeared. 'He's staying away deliberately, just to frighten me,' she muttered crossly, but as the leaden minutes ticked away, and still Bryn did not reappear, a rising tide of fear surmounted her irritation. What if he had slipped and fallen on the steep, rocky slopes? What if he was lying in some defile with a twisted ankle, or worse, a broken leg? She strained her ears to catch a cry for help, but the only sound that assailed them was the endless boom of the combers punishing the rocks on the beach below.

'Where on earth have you been?' He was back, and her pent-up anxiety exploded like a cork from a champagne bottle, venting itself in anger at his unperturbed greeting,

'Hi there! Is there anything new since I've been gone?'

'I sound just like a nagging wife,' Tara realised, aghast.

'You sound just like a nagging wife,' Bryn taunted her with a grin, and she flushed hotly, her cheeks as scarlet as the colour of her skirt, and she hung back, rebuffed, as Meli and Paul and the fisherfolk crowded round Bryn, chattering excitedly, exclaiming as he eased a bulging hand net from off his shoulder and set it gently on to the ground at their feet.

'Dinner,' he announced grandly. 'Or it will be,

when the birds are plucked, and we've made a fire to grill them by.'

'Birds?' Curiosity overcame Tara, and she craned forward with the others to see what it was the net contained.

'How did you manage to catch these?' Paul reached down eager hands to the net.

'I netted them,' Bryn answered him casually. 'It was no different from catching wild turkeys on the range at home. They were feeding on the berried scrub, and the hand net made an ideal trap to drop over them.' He returned the net to its owner with a smile of thanks, outmatched by the latter's grateful grin as he received back his property with a bonus of several birds with which to feed his people.

'I suppose the cactus plants are for table decoration?' Tara regarded the other half of his load with unconcealed disgust. The birds must have been heavy enough to carry, so why add to the burden by bringing in a lot of useless cactus plants? 'A coconut shell of drinking water would have been of more use to us,' she criticised.

'This particular species of cactus contains water,' Bryn informed her evenly. 'The plant stores it for its own use against a period of drought, and it's quite drinkable, in an emergency.'

'But that's wonderful!' Meli cried admiringly. 'I didn't think the mountain slopes on this side were capable of providing us with anything worthwhile in the way of food and drink, and now you've brought us the makings of a feast. How did you know . . .?'

'By experience,' Bryn smiled. 'Work on a ranch often takes a man away from the home station for weeks at a time, and it's necessary to be self-sufficient, and to learn to live off the land in case things go wrong, and you run out of supplies.' His eyes linked with Tara's as he said it, and she stared back at him, gnawing her lower lip uncertainly. Bryn had described himself as 'a sort of cowhand' and she had not believed him. And now he had spoken in the same vein again, although still not directly answering her question, she realised with growing frustration.

'No different from catching wild turkeys on the range at home,' he had said, and, 'work on a ranch,' sketching in a vague background, and leaving her to draw her own conclusions.

'I told you, and you didn't believe me.' His eyes read her thoughts and jeered at her uncertainty, uncaring whether she believed him or not.

'Let's hope your vast experience has taught you how to cook the birds, as well as how to catch them,' she responded tartly, nettled by his attitude.

'All that's needed is a good hot fire,' he answered promptly. 'Paul and I will go and collect some of the scrub for fuel, while you pluck the birds.' He held up a brace and swung them towards her, and Tara recoiled with widening eyes.

'P-pluck them?' she stammered incredulously. 'I couldn't!' She shuddered her revulsion at the mere suggestion. 'I wouldn't have the first notion how to begin,' she added defensively. Her only previous acquaintance with defunct game had been on a plate, flanked by sauce and stuffing, and the mere idea of touching the limp bodies filled her with horror.

'Those who share the work, share the food.' The steel in Bryn's voice warned Tara that the reverse would apply, and she bridled angrily, but before she could speak Meli butted in.

'I'll pluck them—I've done one before, so I know how.'

'You're excused fatigues,' Bryn refused her firmly. 'You've got your hands full with the baby. Paul and I, *and Tara*, will share the chores between us.' He emphasised 'and Tara,' and her lips thinned ominously.

'I won't give in and take the birds from him,' she vowed irefully. 'He can hold them out to me for as long as he chooses!' He was bound to give in and allow his arm to drop some time. No muscles, however tough, could endure the strain of holding out such a weight at arm's length indefinitely. But Bryn's muscles appeared to be made of steel, and his tanned arm remained steadfastly horizontal, challenging her defiance, and to take or not to take the birds suddenly became a fierce contest of wills, fought out in angry silence as their glances met and clashed like drawn swords over the limp feathered bodies dangling like a flag of battle between them.

'Pluck them yourself,' Tara's eyes mutinied. 'I won't back down and take them, not for you, not for anybody!'

'Please yourself,' his answering look signalled back. Did she imagine it, or did his shoulders move in the slightest suggestion of a shrug? She could not be sure, and his arm did not waver or the birds would have swung in his hand, and instead they remained still, remorselessly dangling in front of her, waiting for her to reach out and take them.

'Pluck them, or go hungry.' His hard eyes, the rock-like set of his jaw, made his message plain, and Tara longed to shout back at him,

'Pluck them yourself, I'd rather starve!' and fling away and leave him standing with the birds still dangling, ridiculously, because she would no longer be there for him to dangle them in front of. Impulsively she opened her mouth to shout her defiance in his face, she even half turned to fling away, then her legs gave her an unmistakable warning, as clear as Bryn's own. They shook, and as if to reinforce their urgent message her stomach echoed a hollow plaint. Outnumbered, Tara wavered. With a hunted expression on her face she glanced downwards at the water still surging over the beach.

'It'll be another forty-eight hours before it recedes,' Bryn defined her thoughts, and answered them unasked.

Forty-eight hours. She could not possibly go without food for another day, let alone twice that length of time. If she did she would surely faint, and then she would not be able to walk round the island to seek shelter with Paul and Meli when eventually they returned home. When the time came for her to make the journey Paul would be occupied in looking after Meli and the baby, and would have no time for her, and in her weakness she might be forced to beg Bryn for his help. The possibility was unthinkable, and she rocked back on her heels, torn by indecision. The birds still hung steadfastly in their former position, and she gave them a baleful glare.

'I don't know how to start,' she capitulated grudgingly, and hated Bryn with a fierce hatred for obliging her to give in.

'Begin with the breast feathers, they're the easiest.' To her astonishment he forbore to gloat. Instead he lowered the birds to the ground between them and became briskly practical. 'It's best to pluck a bird while it's still warm.' If he noticed Tara's grimace of distaste he gave no sign, but laid one of the birds so that the soft down of the breast was exposed to his fingers.

'Take the feathers and give them a sharp pull in the direction in which they grow. Like this,' he demonstrated. 'Don't try to pull too many at a time or you'll make your fingers sore, and don't tug them in the opposite direction to the way they grow, or you'll tear the flesh.' The possibility made Tara cringe, and ensured as nothing else could that she would obey his instructions to the letter. 'If I accidentally tear the bird, I'll probably be sick,' she decided shudderingly.

'The fishermen's wives are halfway through plucking

their birds already.' Cruelly he compared her own shrinking incompetence with the busy skill of the other women, around whom feathers flew like floating confetti.

'Now you take over while I go and help Paul to collect fuel for a fire.' Bryn showed her no mercy. The moment he had plucked a mere inch clear of feathers he desisted, waiting only to make sure she continued the work for him.

'You needn't stand over me,' she snapped irritably. 'I won't hand the job to Meli the moment your back's turned, if that's what you're afraid of.'

'I'm not,' he assured her crisply. 'That is,' he added significantly, 'that is if you're as hungry as I think you are.'

'You . . . atishoo!' An unbearable tickle assailed the end of her nose, and completely destroyed the impact of her retort.

'Oh, I forgot to mention,' there was an unconcealed grin on his face that made Tara long to slap him, 'I forgot to mention, it isn't wise to hold your head over the bird while you're plucking it, or the fine down from underneath the feathers will blow in your face and make you sneeze.'

'Beast!' Tara hissed through gritted teeth. 'You didn't forget. You knew, and you let me . . .' But Bryn was already out of earshot, taking the hillside with lithe, distance-consuming strides that made light of the steepness of the slope, and Tara turned her wrath on the hapless birds instead, and began to pluck with a concentrated fury as if it was Bryn and not the birds beneath her flying fingers. The birds were comparatively small, but the feathers seemed to go on for ever. Her fingers were sore and her patience exhausted, but she stuck doggedly to her task. Bryn should not have an opportunity to criticise her performance when he returned.

'I've finished.'

He reappeared with Paul, dragging mounds of brushwood, and Tara got to her feet and waved the naked brace triumphantly in his face. Her fingers felt raw from pulling feathers, but anger drove them on until both the birds were plucked, and she herself was coated from head to toe in fine down. It clung like summer snow to her dark hair, made pale patterns against the scarlet cotton of her skirt, and rested in a soft heap at her feet.

'I've finished.'

Not for the world would she admit to Bryn the glow of achievement that the claim afforded her. Her chin tilted in an independent gesture. He would be doing her no favour by providing her with food, she told herself proudly, she had earned the right to eat by the work of her own hands.

'Well done!' Astonishingly he commended her efforts, and Tara stared at him speechlessly, non-plussed by his unexpected praise. 'I'll take the birds and do the rest.' He took them from her nerveless fingers. She did not enquire what 'the rest' might be. For the sake of her already queasy imagination, she did not want to know. 'Go and shake the down off you before it makes you sneeze again,' he told her, and the glint in his eyes teased her, warming her cheeks. Abruptly she turned away to hide them.

'Not that way, or the wind will blow the feathers back all over us.' He pointed her in the opposite direction, towards an open space where she could rid herself of the feathers in comfort, and she brushed and shook, taking her time in cleaning herself of the clinging down, using the delay to allow her colour to return to normal again before she rejoined the others, despising herself for the warm glow that basked in Bryn's approval.

'If I'm not careful, I'll be thanking him for teaching

me how to do the job,' she told herself disgustedly, but the glow persisted nevertheless, matched by the glow from the brushwood fire that was burning merrily by the time she returned.

'That's burned up quickly,' she voiced her surprise at the speed at which the wood had already begun to redden.

'Thank our range hand here,' Paul jerked his head in Bryn's direction. 'He used the feathers to light the brushwood, and it went up like tinder. If that's not utilising all your resources, I don't know what is. He's a useful fellow to have around in an emergency,' he declared admiringly.

Bryn was a dangerous fellow to have around at any time so far as she herself was concerned, Tara thought ruefully. Perhaps it was the danger that spiced the meat, when later Bryn removed it sizzling from the roughly constructed spit.

'Not exactly Cordon Bleu, but. . . .' He cut a generous portion of the breast and held it out towards Tara, speared on the point of his knife blade. Her mouth watered at the delicious aroma, and she reached out eagerly to take it in her fingers.

'Ooh, it's hot!' Her fingertips, already sore from plucking feathers, jerked away from this further abuse, and tears of pain and frustration welled in her eyes.

'Poor little hands!' Bryn took them in one of his own and regarded the redness of her fingertips with a compassionate look that threatened to make the tears spill over. She blinked rapidly, forcing them back, shrinking from the humiliation of allowing him to see her cry.

'Leave the meat on the blade, and take the knife and eat it from that. Mind your mouth on the point, though,' he cautioned her, 'it's very sharp, and you don't want the pain of cut lips to add to your troubles.'

A cut seemed an insignificant pain for her lips to

endure after the ecstasy and the agony of Bryn's kisses, that left them bruised and trembling still. To hide their weakness from him Tara reached out to take the knife, and the trembling took possession of her hand as well when his fingers closed over her own, making sure her grip on the handle was firm, and in the process nearly destroying her grip on herself. With an immense effort she called on her pride to sustain her, and relied on instinct to steer the meat to her mouth, taking over the task of her hopelessly blurred sight. She bit, and the hot, savoury meat filled her mouth, surpassing any meat she had ever eaten before. She chewed and swallowed and bit again, and felt steadier as the meat on the knife grew gradually smaller and her hunger correspondingly less. Eating meat skewered on a sharp knife blade was a bit like being with the knife's owner, she reflected moodily; the temptation to eat was there, but to satisfy her hunger she had to run the gauntlet of the ever-present danger of sharp pain lurking hidden beneath the surface, ready to cut and wound. The analogy reminded her of the coral reef, and the fate of the *Roseanne*, and she shut her mind sharply to the unwelcome comparison, and cautiously lifted the remains of the cooled meat from off the point of the knife blade, using careful fingers to transfer the food to her mouth that by this means remained triumphantly unharmed. If only she could find such a simple answer to her relationship with Bryn! she wished wistfully.

'More meat?'

'No, thanks, I've had enough.' Her hunger was satisfied on that count at least, and she handed the knife back to Bryn, careful this time to avoid contact with his fingers.

'Wash it down with a drink of cactus wine,' he quipped, and used the blade to slit one of the cactus stems. 'Take it like this.' He held the cut plant above his head and allowed the liquid to trickle down into his open mouth. 'That way, none of it will be wasted.'

The water had a peculiar, brackish taste, but Tara was too thirsty to bother about niceties, and she slaked her parched throat gratefully before the supply ran out.

'With a bit of luck the sea will have receded sufficiently by breakfast time tomorrow for us to draw fresh water from the spring in the rock, and we can catch enough fish in the tide pools to keep us going until we can get to the other side of the island.'

'Breakfast?' Tara exclaimed. 'Surely the day hasn't gone already?' She glanced at her watch.

'It's nearly sunset,' Bryn supplied.

'It'll be a showy sky tonight, after all that happened today,' Meli guessed. 'It was a good sunset last night, wasn't it, Tara?' she probed mischievously.

'Spectacular,' Tara lied, and avoided Bryn's eyes, uncomfortably conscious of her rising colour that must betray to Meli's twinkling glance the reason she had not seen last night's sunset.

'We'll sit and watch it tonight, and see how it compares,' Bryn put in gravely, and Tara's eyes flew, startled, to his face, and met the faint uptilting of his well-cut lips, and the slight, ever so slight, drooping of one eyelid that formed a bond of conspiracy between them, a cosy, intimate alliance to confound Meli's teasing curiosity, and keep their secret intact between themselves.

'Yes, let's.' Suddenly her dark mood vanished, and a gay laugh bubbled from her lips, setting the seal on their conspiracy. She hugged their oneness to herself like a precious secret, and settled on the hard rock beside Bryn as if it was one of the best seats in a theatre box, to watch the day have its last colourful fling, savouring every second to the full because it, too, was something which they shared. No matter that the sunset heralded a night spent in the open, on an inhospitable mountain slope, the fact that Bryn was there too made it safer to Tara than any roof above her head. No matter that she had lost the caravanette, and all her belongings, and that across the wild waters of the bay she could see the *Roseanne*, impaled on coral fangs below the surface, a silent warning to her to beware the folly of dropping her guard—in her new mood of recklessness, Tara discounted these un-important things, and grasped at the fleeting minutes, and the equally fleeting beauty, with hands that were sore from their latent task, heedless that her heart might soon be sorer still when the afterglow faded and the euphoria died in the harsh reality of what breakfast time tomorrow morning might bring.

'We'll keep the fire stoked up.' The colours vanished at last and darkness claimed the sky, and Bryn stretched cramped limbs and began to pile brushwood on the glowing embers of the fire.

'What do we need a big fire for?' Tara watched him uneasily, the first chill touch of reality already reaching out icy fingers to tear aside the frail bond between them. 'Is it to keep away. . .?' She stopped, her eyes apprehensive in the pale heart shape of her face.

'It's to keep away the night chill, not wild animals.' Bryn's face was shadowed in the flickering flames, his expression unreadable, and his tone conveyed nothing of what he thought of her craven fears.

'I only wondered,' she began defensively.

'The largest wild creatures on the island are goats, and they'll steer well clear of us, but the chill from the water won't. The rocks won't hold the heat for long, and we're none of us adequately clothed. Without the fire, we'd be chilled to the bone before morning.' He stoked the fire until it was blazing to his satisfaction, then turned to Tara and suggested,

'Find yourself a comfortable spot and settle down. Paul and I will take it in turns to keep the fire replenished during the night.' His voice was impersonal, the cosy alliance broken, and Tara shivered, although the night air had not yet had time to cool.

'Comfortable?' she echoed scornfully. Bryn did not say where he intended to sit, and she refused to lower her pride to ask him.

'Sit on the brushwood.' He kicked a pile of it together to provide her with a seat.

'It's scratchy,' she objected.

'Better to risk being scratched than to get a chill,' he shrugged. 'The less of you that actually comes into direct contact with the ground, the warmer you'll remain.'

'I suppose that comes from your range experience as well?' she remarked sourly, but his advice made sense, and she lowered herself gingerly on to the brushwood pile.

'Ooh!' Sharp bits stuck in, and with a pained expression on her face she used urgent hands to push the most intrusive of the sticks out of the way.

'Wriggle yourself a comfortable spot.' There was an undisguised laugh in Bryn's voice as he viewed her predicament, and Tara's glare became vitriolic.

'Don't keep on harping about comfort,' she snapped. 'Comfort was my bunk in the van, and by now that's at the bottom of the bay.' Reality returned with a vengeance, and she could not control the shake in her voice as she contemplated the fate of the caravanette. 'Brushwood makes a poor pillow,' she complained to hide it.

'Try me as a substitute.'

He answered her unasked question, and confounded her complaint, and with one lithe movement he dropped on to the brushwood pile beside her and picked her up and drew her on to his knee, leaning her back against him, using his own body to protect her from the sharp points of the sticks. Too surprised by his unexpected move to make any resistance, Tara remained quiescent against him, and he spoke.

'Is that more comfortable?' he asked the top of her head softly.

'Mmm.' It was heaven, but pride demanded that she must not tell him so.

'Then go to sleep, you'll need all the rest you can get, because it's likely to be a strenuous day tomorrow. Goodnight, Tara.'

It was dark, and she was exhausted, but she was still alert enough to discern the brush of his lips against her hair. Every soft dark curl signalled an electric message at his touch, and Tara crouched breathlessly still in his arms, longing to reach up and press his head down to meet her lips, longing to give rein to the eager response that clamoured for expression at the feel of his kiss. She gave a small, convulsive movement in his arms, but the sight of Paul and Meli hard by checked her, and she lay back again in her former position, and Bryn's arms tightened round her, holding her still as he murmured,

'Sleep tight.'

It was impossible. He might as well suggest she fly to the moon. Sleep was about as far away. She felt wide awake and wonderfully, vitally alive. Her heart pounded—surely Bryn must feel it with his arms so close about her? She could feel the throb of his against her cheek, and every nerve end of her vibrated to the strong, live rhythm of it. Sleep? Impossible!

She slept.

CHAPTER SEVEN

THE steady drumbeat of Bryn's heart changed tempo, and became a continuous rumble. Tara could not pinpoint the moment when it began, but it seemed to go on for a long time, and she stirred uneasily in her sleep. The slight movement brought her ribs into contact with something thin and sharp-ended, that stuck in painfully. Bryn's knife? Perhaps he had it in his pocket when she went to sleep? She sent complaining fingers to push it away, and they encountered not a knife, but a stick end. The rumble became a roar, and her eyes flew open, wide with fright.

'Bryn?'

She rolled over, and more sticks stuck in, prodding her fully awake. Bryn was gone, and she was lying full length on the brushwood pile instead of on his lap, and a loud sucking, roaring sound like the noise of an express train rushing through a narrow tunnel rattled in her ears and vibrated through her body, coming from above her, and underneath her, and. . . . Regardless of the sticks, she jerked upright.

'Bryn?' Her voice was shrill with fear. The last roar had been a tidal wave that chased them across the beach and up the hillside. Had they come high enough? Was this another, bigger wave than before? The roar was equally loud, but somehow different. More concentrated. More terrifying. The ground shook beneath her.

'Bryn?' Terror rolled her off the brushwood couch and on to her feet.

'Over here, Tara!' Bryn's voice called to her

through the darkness, and blindly she stumbled
towards it. A hand reached out, and she grasped it,
and even in the darkness she knew that it was Bryn's
hand, and she clung to it with both her own as he
drew her towards him, towards the group of people
with him. Silent people. Paul and Meli, and the
fisherfolk, all huddled together, and staring upwards,
eerily quiet. She became aware of something else.

'The sunset's come back,' she discovered in a
puzzled voice. She blinked up at the reddened sky
with eyes that were still stupid with sleep. There
should not be two sunsets in one day. She had sat
beside Bryn and watched the colours fade from the
sky, how many hours ago? And now, unaccountably,
they were back again.

'It isn't the sunset. It's a reflection from inside the
crater above us.' Bryn's voice was grave, and ominously
calm. Sleep fled, and Tara's eyes flew upwards to
search his face. The ruddy glow from the sky
illumined his features, etching them with fire,
heightening her first imaginative impression of him as
a fair-haired Vulcan. Crystallising her fear.

'The crater's dead!' Her voice rose, and her eyes
became wide pools of dread, begging him to set her
fears at naught. 'The volcano's extinct. Paul said. . . .'
She gulped to a halt.

'The volcano's been *dormant* for over a century.' His
emphasis underlined the fine point of difference, and
Tara swallowed on a throat that was suddenly
incapable of speech. 'The eruption that sent in the
tidal wave must have jolted it into life again.'

Noisy life. Fearsome life. The slopes beneath her
feet vibrated with the thunderous growls of the giant's
awakening, while clouds of smoke and tongues of
flame belched from the crater like an angry dragon.

'Aaah!' A groan broke the silence of the watching
group, and Tara's hand tightened convulsively about

Bryn's fingers as the crater above them boiled over. The rumbles increased in intensity, and the tongues of flame became a fountain, flinging fiery plumes hundreds of feet into the sky, thrusting aside the darkness, and staining the earth as well as the clouds in a weird, satanic glow. Red serpents of fire wriggled over the black rocks that lined the crater's rim and began to pour down the mountainside.

Lava! Tara stared up at it with dilated eyes.

'All the old lava flows come down on this side of the mountain!' she realised with a thrill of horror. Frantically she turned on Bryn. 'We must get away! Now, before it's too late. Back to the beach. . . .'

'The sea's still covering the beach.' He cut her short harshly. 'There's no escape that way.' The constant booming of the combers confirmed the truth of his words, a threatening accompaniment to the ominous rumblings from the mountain.

'The canoes. . . .' Then she remembered, there were no canoes. The tidal wave had smashed them to matchwood, and there was no wood among the scrub on the slopes that could be lashed together to make a raft, let alone a canoe, even if they had time. Tara glanced fearfully upwards and saw that the glowing snakes of lava had already doubled in length.

'We're trapped.'

Trapped between a steadily approaching flow of red hot, molten rock from above, and the wild, storm lashed water below. Trapped. The word hammered to and fro in Tara's brain in a crescendo of terror, and she beat at Bryn with agonised fists.

'The lava doesn't flow down the other side of the mountain. If you'd left me under the palm trees, I'd be safe!'

'Stop it, Tara. Stop it!' He took her by the shoulders and shook her without mercy, cutting off her rising hysteria, and rendering her breathless so that no more words could come, only gasping sobs that shuddered through her shaking frame.

'It'll be daylight in an hour or so,' Paul began.

'We can't wait for daylight before we move,' Bryn said grimly. 'Look above you, to the left. The lava's breaking out of the clefts in the mountainside, as well as from the crater at the top.' He pointed, and Tara caught her breath as she followed the direction of his arm. Smoke and steam and fiery lava spewed from a gaping cleft halfway down the mountainside towards them, just such a cleft from which Bryn had picked the sprig of maidenhair fern to go with her ohia blossom. There would be no fern left growing in the cleft now, nor anything else in the lava's destructive path, Tara saw with a shiver. An ominous crackling joined the other noises of the night as the leading tongues of red set the scrub on fire in front of it, pushing a curtain of smoke and flames downwards across the mountainside. Downwards, in their direction. Sulphur fumes blew rank on the wind, and Tara began to cough.

'The lava from the clefts will reach us in half the time of the lava from the crater itself.' Paul's voice was hoarse.

'So, we don't stand around and wait for it,' Bryn responded promptly.

'But the beach . . . you said. . . .'

'The beach is out,' he stated adamantly. 'We'll have to keep to the side of the mountain and work our way across it, and onto the bluff of rock that thrusts out into the sea. It's our only chance. The bluff should be the last place to feel the lava, and by the time it becomes a threat there the water should have receded sufficiently for us to climb down to the beach on the other side of the bluff, and make our way to the windward side of the island, and safety. That is, if the lava flows take the same direction as they did before.'

There was no guarantee that they would, and the uncertainty sent Tara cold with dread.

'Everybody link hands and form a chain.' Once more Bryn took charge, and this time Tara was too frightened to resent his authority. 'Put each child between two adults,' he spoke directly to the fisherman who understood English. 'Paul, you and Meli and I will walk abreast. That way we can each keep one arm round Meli, and help her along.' He said nothing to Tara, and she felt herself go deathly still. Even in extremis she found herself waiting, hoping, for some word from Bryn for her alone, some sign that she was not merely one of the crowd to him.

'Tara, take hold of my belt at the back with your one hand, and grasp the next one in line with your other.' He spoke, placing her next in line to himself, giving her something of himself to hold on to. Using her as his link-pin with the rest of the line. The small trust warmed her, and she grasped his belt eagerly, feeling the firm, supple leather of it beneath her fingertips, warm from the contact with his body. She would rather have held his hand, but the belt was next best, and confidence flowed back, taking the shake from her limbs. He brought it back with his next words.

'Don't let go of one another.' He raised his voice so that the fisherman who understood English could hear him, and interpret for his people. 'There'll be no time to go back to look for anyone who strays from the line. Carry the smaller children, and we'll keep our pace down to what the others are capable of. There's no time to lose.'

The straggling line reminded Tara irresistibly of a crocodile of schoolchildren clutching towels and bathing costumes, on their way to the local baths for their weekly swimming lesson, but there the likeness ended. Then, she had wanted to dawdle, to spin out the walk and postpone their destination and the lesson. Now, she wanted to run. Every instinct screamed that she must fly while she still could, away from the inferno of fire and smoke and fumes that poured in an evil wave down the mountain slopes above them, blowing choking clouds of hot cinders on the gusting wind.

'Nature's demolition squad.' Her lips twisted as she remembered Bryn's description. A hurricane, a tidal wave, and now a volcanic eruption. Even Bryn could not have foreseen with what thoroughness the squad would set to work.

The rough scrub whipped against her legs, sharp and scratching. Too late she wished she had put on slacks instead of a skirt, a torn, ragged skirt that did even less than it might to protect her shrinking skin. Perspiration ran down her face, blinding her eyes. It dropped off her chin, and soaked the palms of her hands. The rough, rocky surface of the mountainside caught at her feet, laughing at her futile attempt to escape its fury. The weird red light from the crater flickered and died and rose again, throwing long shadows, so that one minute she could see the way ahead, and the next, nothing. She stumbled on an unseen rock, and her perspiration-wet hand slipped from its grip on Bryn's belt.

'Tara?' He checked instantly, and half turned.

'My hand slipped.' She raised eyes that were dazed with weariness, and her voice came out as a harsh croak. Croaking an excuse, to defend herself from Bryn. She felt too tired for self-contempt to register. She drew her free hand across her eyes, then used it to grope forward, reaching for a fresh grip on his belt.

'Keep going, I've got you.' Steel fingers circled her wrist, pulling her on. He held her. He no longer trusted her to hold him. She had failed him as his link-pin. Misery at her failure made the thorns of the brush

sharper, the rocks rougher. Bryn had asked of her one
thing, and she had failed him. Irrational guilt rode her
exhausted mind, transcending even the terror of the
volcano, and she longed to creep away and hide, but
the hand that held her from behind clung to her
fingers like a limpet, and Bryn's hold round her wrist
pulled her remorselessly forward, and she staggered
on, gasping and choking from the wind-driven smoke
and fumes and cinders through a night that would
never end.

The air was suddenly clearer, more breatheable, and
a faint mist hung on the wind, a cool restorative over
her face and hands. Tara raised her eyes and
discovered she could see around her. It was daylight.
And they were on the wide causeway of rocks reaching
out into the water. The sea, and not the mountain, was
on either side of them.

'Loose hands now, and rest.' Bryn loosed her wrist,
and Tara dropped to the ground, Meli dropped beside
her, and Paul transferred the baby from his arms to
her lap. Incredibly, the infant slept.

'He's packed enough adventure into the last forty-
eight hours to last him a lifetime,' Bryn smiled.

'So have you,' Paul responded grimly. 'Look at your
yacht, it's settled lower in the water than it was last
night. It seems to be tilted at a sharper angle, too.'

'The reef's holed it.' Bryn cast his erstwhile
possession an unemotional look. 'It's probably half full
of water by now, from the constant battering of the
combers. It's only a matter of time before the weight
pulls it off the reef and sinks it,' he surmised.

How could he be so unemotional about his yacht?
Tara stared at him in amazement. She had felt distress
at the loss of the caravanette, and it was only a hired
vehicle. True, most of her concern came from worry
as to her financial liability for the loss of the van, but
Bryn showed no signs of worry on that score, either.

The wages of present-day cowhands must be phenom-
enal, to allow him to view it so coolly, she decided
caustically. And Bryn himself must be as hard as the
coral reef, to remain so unmoved about the loss of a
vessel named *Roseanne*. Named after whom?

She became aware of his eyes resting upon her face,
reading the changing expression there. Reading her
thoughts? Hastily she switched them off, and burst
into speech to cover her confusion.

'You look as if you've just come out of a coalmine!'
The sight of his face gave her a quick lead. Black
streaks lined his skin, smudged where trickles of
perspiration trekked across the grime. His hair was
dulled by a layer of cinder dust, and his once white
shirt and shorts were liberally patterned with black.

'You too.' Briefly his teeth flashed white against the
grime, and for the first time Tara became aware of her
own dishevelled state. Her blouse reflected the state of
Bryn's clothes. Her arms and legs echoed the smears
on his, and if her face was in the same state. . . .

'It is.' His quick grin read her thoughts and
answered them, and her eyes flew instinctively to the
showers of spray rearing up over the top of the nearby
rocks.

'Don't.' He divined her intention, and immediately
countermanded it.

'I don't see why not,' she bridled.

'We don't know how long we'll have to wait to have
a wash in clear water. The salt in the spray could make
your skin sore if it's left on for too long.' Then, as he
saw her hesitate, his voice hardened, and he shrugged.
'Take your choice between a dirty face and a sore one,'
he finished indifferently.

'We ought to be like those goats over there,' Meli
said enviously. 'The dirt doesn't show on their black
coats. They can shake themselves and get rid of the
dust easily enough.'

'They're tamer than the goat we saw on the mountain.' Tara followed Meli's gaze to where a small herd of about a dozen animals, with a large black billygoat at their head, stood outstaring them from the rocks on the other side of the bluff. 'The one we saw, fled the moment he caught sight of the caravanette.'

'I've never known them to come so close,' Meli observed. 'They're normally very shy. Perhaps they're more afraid of the mountain than they are of us,' she guessed compassionately.

'More afraid of the mountain. . . .' Bryn echoed, and gave the goats a long, considering look. 'I wonder?' He broke off, then resumed in a casual voice, 'I think I'll go across to the other side of the bluff, and find out what drove them in this direction.'

'I'll come with you.' Something in Bryn's voice drove Tara to his side. Whatever it was he wanted to find out, she wanted to know about it too.

'There's no need,' he said discouragingly.

'I'm coming anyway,' she stated adamantly. 'I want to stretch my legs.' As an excuse it did not hold water. The muscles of her legs were already overstretched, and stiff and weary from their flight across the mountain, their skin scratched and sore from contact with the abrasive scrub.

'As you please.' He made no further objection, and she fell in beside him and walked without speaking towards the far rocks. Erratic explosions sounded from somewhere over the lip of the bluff, and a peculiar loud hissing sound became even louder the further they walked, joining forces with the surf and the noises from the mountain to fill the silence between them. Bryn broke it first.

'The goats aren't moving.' He watched the unusual behaviour of the animals with keen eyes.

'Let's steer well clear of them,' Tara begged. 'It's a shame to frighten them any more.' She refused to admit that the sight of the large black billygoat frightened her far more than she probably frightened it. A pair of baleful yellow eyes fixed her unwinkingly from the rocks ahead, and she veered nervously to one side of the small herd.

'This is far enough, I should be able to see all I need from here.' Bryn took her by the hand and pulled her with him to the top of a large outcrop of rock some distance away from the one occupied by the goats. 'From this height we should be able to get a clear view of the beach on the windward side of the island.' The beach where she had first parked her van under the coconut palms. The beach. . . .

'There isn't a beach any longer!' Tara's eyes widened as she gazed downwards to where the beach had once been. 'There aren't any coconut palms, either.' Water as wild as the bay on the leeward side rolled and boomed and sprayed over the spot where, only days before, she had lazed on coral sand. Clouds of steam hissed from the edge of the water, giving it the appearance of a witches' cauldron. Bryn had described it as a cauldron, she remembered.

'Those awful bangs!' A veritable fusillade of explosions sent her hands to cover her protesting ears. 'And the steam. . . .'

'The explosions are the rocks bursting under the heat of the lava flow, and the steam is coming from where the red hot lava meets the waves.'

Then she saw it, the thing that the clouds of steam from the water's edge had hidden from her sight, the lava flow that covered the hillside as far as she could see on the windward side of the island, reaching from the crater at the top of the mountain, to the water's edge below. The lush vegetation and the green forest where she had plucked the frangipani blossoms for the van lay waste under the grey writhing mass of molten rock, through which spears of fiery red broke continuously, sending heat waves shimmering across the inexorably moving surface until the whole mountain appeared to writhe in some evil dance.

'There's no way we can cross that,' Bryn said gravely. 'It must extend for several miles across the side of the mountain.'

Cutting off their escape route to the other side of the island. Marooning them on the bluff of rocks that suddenly seemed to Tara's frightened eyes to shrink to half their size. What if the lava flow. . . .

'We're cut off.' Her voice was a thin thread of fear.

'Not quite. There *is* a way.'

'It had better be a quick one.' Paul joined them and scanned the scene of devastation on the other side of the island with eyes that reflected Tara's dismay. 'We've neither food nor water, and no means of getting hold of either along this bluff. How . . .?' he asked hopefully.

'The *Roseanne*,' Bryn said quietly, nodding to his stricken yacht on the leeward side of the bluff.

'The yacht's out of reach,' Paul's voice criticised Bryn for raising false hopes. 'It'd be suicide to attempt to reach it, in seas as wild as this.' He shook his head firmly. 'On the rocks of the bluff, we do stand a chance, even if it's a slim one.'

'The *Roseanne*'s got a wireless,' Bryn insisted. 'If I could manage to reach the yacht, and the wireless is still working, I could send out a Mayday call for help.'

'Even if you managed to reach the yacht, the radio might be out of action,' Paul objected.

'If it's out of action, there are the distress flares,' Bryn persisted. 'I've been watching the combers, Paul,' he warmed to his theme enthusiastically, 'the rocks on the end of the bluff here turn the waves straight towards the yacht, which is why they're giving it such a hammering now. See how the combers swing outwards from the bluff, and break over the deck of the *Roseanne*,' he pointed.

'So?' Paul's doubt showed in his face and his voice.

'I reckon if I could choose the right moment, and a big enough comber,' Bryn pursued, 'I could body-surf myself on to the deck of the yacht.'

'Get smashed against the side of it, more likely,' Paul objected, but there was a light of hope in his eyes, and seeing it, Tara burst into urgent speech.

'You mustn't even contemplate it!' She turned on Bryn frantically. 'I won't allow you to try. Stop him, Paul,' she begged the other man. 'It's a crazy idea—you know it and I know it. Convince Bryn, before it's too late,' she beseeched him. All the antagonism, all the resentment, fled, and pride went with them. Only Bryn remained, and if he was allowed to carry out his wild, quixotic plan.... 'You'll never reach the yacht,' she sobbed. 'I'd rather remain here with you and take my chance with the mountain.' With clinging hands she held him by the forearms and shook them in her desperation to get her message across. 'You said yourself the yacht might sink at any moment. If you do manage to reach it alive, and then it founders....' She could not go on. Tears coursed unashamed down her cheeks, washing away the grime, and a strange expression flitted across the man's face as he watched, but her own eyes were too blinded by tears to see. 'Don't attempt it, Bryn,' she entreated him, and knew despairingly that, even as she flung her plea at him, she might as well fling it at the unyielding rock she stood on.

'I've got to try, Tara.' And if trying meant tearing her in two, he would still go ahead.

'I'll come with you,' Paul offered staunchly, and Bryn immediately shook his head.

'Thanks, Paul, but no. This is my job—alone,' he emphasised, and as Paul looked ready to argue he added authoritatively, 'you've got Meli and the baby to consider. I've got no ties.'

And she, Tara, did not count. Tara sent him a stricken look, and her pale cheeks went whiter still as he turned away and threw over his shoulder casually to Paul,

'Your turn will come if I fail.'

'Bryn. . . !' His name was a strangled cry, dredged from the depths of her aching throat, but he heard it and turned back, and her heart beat high with a wild hope. She reached out beseeching hands towards him, and he took them in both his own and held them while his eyes travelled slowly over her face, drinking in each delicate feature. Such blue eyes. They searched her own, probing deep as if trying to impart some message. Tara strained to catch whatever it might be, but it eluded her.

'Tara?' He paused, and she caught her breath. Would he tell her? She tensed, waiting. What would he tell her?

'Wish me luck, Tara.'

'Luck?' He loosed her hands and turned away, and her arms dropped lifelessly to her sides. Luck, against mountainous combers that were pounding his yacht to destruction? Luck, against insuperable odds?

'How like Bryn, to think that he, and no one else, can do it!' Fear turned to anger that he should rack her so, and her anger turned against Bryn. 'It's sheer arrogance, to think that only he can do it!' she choked.

'Hush, Tara!' Paul put a steadying arm round her shoulders, that brought her no comfort. If only it were Bryn's arm, and not Paul's.

'It's true,' she sobbed. 'Bryn thinks he's the only one who can accomplish anything. What about the fishermen? They're locals, and used to the sea.'

'They're all married men, with children.'

And Bryn had no ties. Frozenly Tara watched him climb high on to a rock above the pounding surf. A comber broke below him, and for a second he vanished in a cloud of flying spray, but when it cleared he was still there, watching, waiting, biding his time until a large enough comber came his way, assessing its size, and carrying power.

'Now!'

Paul shouted, and Bryn dived, and the comber careened off the rock and turned straight in line for the *Roseanne*.

'He's gone!' Her hands rose to her throat. She longed to shut her eyes, and could not. She longed to weep, but her eyes were dry. She clung to Paul and lived a lifetime of suspense while she strove fruitlessly to pierce the water where Bryn had disappeared.

'He's surfaced!' Paul's voice was jubilant. 'Look, he's rising with the water, out of the trough.'

'He can't swim in that,' Tara whispered. Human strength, even Bryn's strength, was futile against the power of the sea.

'He won't try,' Paul replied confidently. 'He's body-surfing. Using his body like a surfboard, to ride the crest of the comber,' he explained, when he saw that Tara did not understand.

A slim, pale arrow of a body, challenging a hostile environment. A frail sliver of white against the immense green comber that hurtled with frightening speed towards the side of the *Roseanne*.

'Will the comber be high enough to put him on the deck of the yacht?' Paul muttered anxiously.

Or would it break, and dash him against the side? Tara's frightened mind provided the unspoken alternative, and she twisted her fingers together, her nails biting deep into the palms of her hands. Her teeth bit into her lower lip, and she tasted the raw salt taste of blood, but she was unaware of pain, only aware of Bryn being lifted towards the side of the yacht, riding the great comber like a vast moving stairway. Twenty yards to go, ten, and the tip of the comber began to curl over.

'The wave's beginning to break. He'll never reach the deck.' Unable to watch, she buried her face in Paul's shoulder.

'He's made it, Tara. He's made it!' In an excess of relief Paul lifted her off her feet and swung her round in a crazy jig. 'Bryn's on the deck. Look, Tara! Look!' he exulted.

'He's down. He's not getting up.' Tara looked, and her relief vanished. Through sheets of flying spray she could dimly discern Bryn's figure, spreadeagled across the deck, and another comber, about to break over the *Roseanne*. 'He's dazed. He'll be washed back into the sea!' The comber broke, and the deck disappeared in a deluge of green water. 'Bryn. . . .' she moaned faintly.

'He's getting up. He's all right!' Meli jumped up and down with excitement. She and the fisherfolk had come unnoticed to join Tara and Paul, and watched the drama as tensely as they. 'He must have seen the comber coming, and held on until it passed. Hurray for Bryn!' Meli cried, and a ragged cheer broke from the little group as Bryn pulled himself to his feet, and looked round him as if he was trying to get his bearings. Tara caught her breath as he turned, located the bluff of rock, and raised his hand to signal that all was well. Did he signal to herself, or to Paul, or was it just a general signal to all of them? For the moment Tara did not care. For the moment, Bryn was safe.

'What's he doing now?' Paul questioned anxiously, and Tara strained her eyes to see. 'He seems to have stopped.' Bryn pulled himself hand over hand along the steeply sloping deck, then halted, and seemed to rummage among some anonymous equipment that the driving spray made it impossible for Tara to identify.

'Surely he's not trying to launch the lifeboat on his own? He'll never get it free from the tackle, with the deck tilting at that angle.' Tense minutes passed, minutes during which Tara's stretched nerves reached screaming point. Why did Bryn delay? Each minute that passed heightened his danger while he remained on the yacht.

'He's lighting a distress flare.' Paul's eyes did not battle against the disadvantage of Tara's blurred vision, and he quickly divined Bryn's intention. 'There it goes! And another.' High in the heavens, one after the other, twin cries for help rocketed upwards and flared. Would anyone notice such puny sparks against the spectacular exhibition of the mountain behind them? Despair rose in Tara as she watched the flares arc overhead, and die away.

'The wireless must be out of action.'

'Not necessarily,' Paul comforted her. 'Bryn might have backed it both ways, just in case. See, he's going below.' The flares gone, Bryn clawed his way along the sloping deck and disappeared inside the yacht, to meet who knew what hazards in the flooded lower reaches of the vessel?

The hour that followed was one of the worst of Tara's life. Bryn remained steadfastly out of sight. Working the ship's wireless? Or. . . . She dared not allow her mind to dwell on the alternative, which was too awful to contemplate. The combers continued to batter unceasingly at the yacht, plumes of fire belched from the mountain, and there was nothing she could do except stand and watch, and wait . . . and wait. . . .

'Sit down and rest,' Paul advised her kindly, and she shook her head.

'I can't.' She would know no rest until Bryn was safe. Her own plight on the bluff of rock paled into insignificance beside the dangers that faced Bryn.

'Listen.' Paul raised his head. 'Can you hear something?'

'Hear what?' Tension made Tara irritable. The combined noises from the mountain and the sea were loud enough to drown all other minor sounds. 'What is it I'm expected to hear?' she demanded without interest.

'It sounded like ... it *is!*' Paul's voice rose with excitement. 'It's a helicopter—a Sea King.'

'A—what?' Tara stared at him, uncomprehending.

'A helicopter, over there.' He pointed, and Tara's ears caught the faint mechanical rattle even before she espied the growing speck in the sky that flew purposefully towards them, as if it knew they were on the bluff. As if it had been guided to them.

'Bryn must have got the ship's wireless working. He's managed to send out a Mayday call, and the military have picked it up and sent a helicopter to lift us off the bluff,' Paul diagnosed.

'It may not be looking for us,' Tara objected. 'It may have come to check on the extent of the eruption.'

'No, it's circling,' Paul confirmed, 'it's going to land. Good for Bryn!'

Where was Bryn? Tara could not bring herself to share in the general excitement. Her eyes scanned the wave-lashed deck of the *Roseanne* with growing anxiety. The Mayday call must have gone out from the yacht, because the helicopter had arrived in answer. So why did not Bryn reappear? She strained her eyes to probe the flying spray, but the deck remained obdurately empty. And moving, she realised with a thrill of horror. Slowly, almost imperceptibly, so that at first she was not sure whether it was an illusion, then faster as the crashing waves gave it momentum, the stern of the yacht began to settle deeper into the water. Had Bryn, moving about below, tipped the scales and started the yacht on its final journey to the sea-bed? Pulled by the weight of the water inside, the *Roseanne* began to sink, and Tara held her breath until she felt as if her lungs must burst.

The helicopter landed, and uniformed men appeared, and Paul and Meli and the fisherfolk hurried eagerly to meet them, but Tara was conscious of none of these. Alone, she stood frozenly staring at the yacht. Too numb to cry, she watched the *Roseanne* slip inch by inch further below the surface of the water, until the entire stern end was submerged. Then it stopped moving and seemed to settle, and the bows were left pointing upwards at an acute angle, straight towards the sky.

And still Bryn did not reappear.

CHAPTER EIGHT

'WE'RE ready to lift off, miss.' A pause, then again, with rising impatience, 'We're ready to. . . .'

'You can't go without Bryn.' She had heard him the first time, but her ears refused to accept the sense of what he said.

'Who's Bryn?' The uniformed man looked round him as if he expected to see Bryn appear from behind one of the nearby rocks.

'He's on the yacht. You can't go without him. You'll have to wait.'

'We can't stay here, miss, and that's for sure,' the newcomer declared forthrightly.

'I'm not asking you to wait for long,' Tara begged desperately. 'Only until Bryn gets back.'

'If there's a man on the yacht,' the soldier sent a dubious glance across the seething waters towards the *Roseanne*, 'there's no way he's going to get back on to the bluff to join you. Look at the combers,' he reasoned. 'They're all racing in the direction of the yacht, and nothing but a fish could swim against water like that. Whoever's on the yacht will have to stay there until the other helicopter gets to him.'

'What other helicopter?' Tara echoed bewilderedly. 'Why can't this one. . . .'

'The Sea King's a big transport machine,' the soldier explained patiently. 'There's no place for it to land on the yacht with the deck tilted at that angle, and if there was, the vessel's half submerged already, and the weight of the 'copter would probably push the rest of it right under the water. The Sea King's not equipped for rescue work, the other helicopter is, and they'll be able to send a man down on a line. They're only half an hour or so behind us,' he coaxed.

'Half an hour? That might be too late,' Tara moaned despairingly. 'The yacht's sinking. It slid further under the water a few minutes ago while I was watching. We can't just go away and leave him there—desert him,' she choked to a standstill.

'What I can see of the yacht looks stable enough to me.' The serviceman took her by the arm and began to propel her purposefully towards the Sea King, where a queue of patient fisherfolk waited their turn to climb aboard.

'It moved, I tell you,' Tara insisted, and tried in vain to pull free from his hold. 'I saw it!' She looked round desperately for Paul to help her, but he was already helping Meli into the aircraft, even as she looked the two disappeared inside the machine, along with the fisherman, who carried his net over his shoulder, and two small children, one under each arm. The ones who were left were of no help to her, they looked at her curiously, not understanding her distress because they did not speak English, and there could be no communication between them, while the soldier was already busy helping to carry the remaining children aboard. The pilot's voice sounded from inside the machine, urging haste.

'Up you get, miss.' The soldier returned, and his tone was brisk and commanding, and as Tara hesitated, 'It's pointless you standing here, there's nothing you can do for the yachtsman, and every minute we delay places the lives of the rest of the party at risk,' he blackmailed her.

The rotors clattered overhead, and Tara pressed her face to the window and stared down as the helicopter lifted off the bluff, then turned and swung out over the sea, over the yacht. The bow pointed up at them like an accusing finger, condemning them for abandoning Bryn, and Tara's eyes filled as they scoured the almost vertical deck. Everything moveable had long since disappeared, and only one or two fixtures jutted out from the structure. From the top of one of these, an arm waved.

'Bryn!' Tara stared at it for a moment of pure disbelief, then it waved again, and she spun round excitedly to the soldier sat beside her. 'Bryn's alive! He's waving to us. Surely there's something you can do? Hover above him, and let down a rope or something? The fisherman's got a net,' she clutched at straws. 'Tell the pilot, quickly, before we've gone too far!' she beseeched the man urgently.

'Sit down, miss, do, and calm yourself.' The soldier pressed her back into her seat. 'I've told you, there's nothing we can do. With this machine we can't get close enough to reach the man, we'd risk one of the combers catching the 'copter and crashing it, and I'm not putting the lives of twenty people at risk, for the sake of one.'

The helicopter clattered on its way, inexorably putting more distance between herself and Bryn, more distance between Bryn and safety. Tensely Tara searched the sky for a sight of the promised second helicopter, and after what seemed hours it eventually passed them, heading out in the direction from which they had just come. By the time it passed over the bay, would the yacht still be there for it to find?

'He's been diverted from his routine coastal patrol,' the soldier explained, and Tara heard her own voice reply,

'He must be used to this kind of rescue.'

'Oh yes, he's equipped for it,' the soldier was patently pleased that he had succeeded in diverting her attention, and went on chattily, 'he'll send someone down on a hawser and winch up his man, as easy as picking an apple out of a dish.'

Easy, if the man was still there to be winched up.

The military base was bare and functional, but the occupants made up for it by their friendly hospitality. Within minutes of landing the bedraggled party was ushered into a canteen hut where food and hot, sweet coffee was pressed upon them, but hungry as she was, Tara could not eat, and she took her coffee with her and wandered over to the nearest window, the better to see the rescue helicopter the moment it appeared over the horizon.

'What are you going to do now, Tara?' Meli brought her plate and cup, and joined her.

'Do?' Tara echoed uncomprehendingly. She would wait for Bryn. What else was there to do?

'The military are putting some spare living huts at the disposal of the fisherfolk, until they've decided what they want to do,' Meli explained. 'Paul and I are going to stay with relatives here for a time, until we can find a place of our own. Paul's telephoning them now, and one of the soldiers has promised to take us to their house in a jeep when we're ready. You're very welcome to come with us,' she invited Tara warmly. 'We'll leave as soon as we've eaten.'

'Leave, without seeing Bryn again?' the idea was unthinkable.

'Paul will be in touch with Bryn,' Meli reassured her, 'and we'll all meet up again at the christening,' she promised.

'The jeep's ready whenever you are, ma'am.'

A tall, gangling young soldier, wearing working denims and an engaging smile, stopped in front of Meli, and she rose and settled the baby more comfortably in the crook of her arm.

'Do come with us, Tara,' she urged again.

'I can't.' Tara's voice was flat.

'But where will you go? What will you do?' Meli was plainly perplexed by her refusal. 'You've lost your caravanette, your clothes, your passport. . . .'

Even the caravanette seemed of small importance now, only Bryn. She had to wait and make sure he was all right before she committed herself.

'I'll think of something. I must wait and see Bryn land first,' she excused herself lamely.

'You won't have long to wait.' Paul pointed upwards, and Tara's heart missed a beat as a distant speck in the sky turned into a helicopter, which hovered and sank to the ground only yards away from the hut. The door of the machine opened and a figure in uniform appeared.

'Bryn's not with them!' Fear sent Tara as cold as ice, and the hut went dark before her eyes, then through the darkness a patch of white appeared behind the man in uniform, and Bryn's voice, strong and confident, called out to the crew,

'Thanks for the lift. Be seeing you!' He raised a hand to his rescuers and strode towards the hut door, a lithe, easy stride, that bore no signs of injury.

'Bryn!' In an excess of relief Tara ran to meet him, her eyes shining her thankfulness at his safe return. 'Bryn, thank heavens you're safe! I. . . .'

'I see you're all being well looked after.' He divided a cool nod between the room at large, and Tara flinched back as if she had been struck. Briefly his eyes raked her face, and she caught a hard breath. Surely he would say something, some word that was meant for her alone, to say he was glad she was safe, was glad she had waited for him?

'Glad you made it, Paul.' He strolled over to join Paul and Meli by the window, leaving Tara to tag along behind him if she felt so inclined, and anger and bitter resentment at his rebuff fought a war with relief, and won hands down, enabling her to ignore Bryn and station herself independently beside Meli, as Paul said gratefully,

'We made it, thanks to you.'

'We were just lucky the wireless was in working order,' Bryn dismissed his part of the rescue with a shrug, and took a proffered coffee from a soldier.

'Thanks.' He put the cup to his lips, and his blue eyes pierced Tara over its rim, an all-encompassing look that brought swift colour to her cheeks, but still he did not speak until his coffee was finished, then he said,

'How did the baby stand the journey, Meli?'

'Fine,' the young mother smiled, 'he slept all the way.'

Bitterly Tara envied the infant its blissful unconsciousness. Bryn had spoken to both Paul and Meli, and vouchsafed never a syllable to herself. He compounded his transgression by enquiring, 'What are your plans now, Paul?' He was interested in the others' plans, and completely ignored her own.

'If that's how he feels,' Tara told herself angrily, 'he can keep his interest! I don't want it. Once he's discharged his obligation to me for the loss of the caravanette, he can go his way, and I'll go mine, and we need never see one another again,' she fumed, and felt black desolation choke her at the prospect.

'We're going to stay with relatives until we can find a place of our own,' Paul answered.

'And I'm going with them,' Tara declared impulsively. She ignored Meli's look of startled surprise at her complete volte-face and went on brightly, 'It was kind of your relatives to include me in the invitation. It'll give me a few days' breathing space while I sort out things with the British Consul.' Deliberately she turned her back on Bryn and walked beside Meli towards the waiting jeep.

'They'll have to provide us with a bigger vehicle,' Meli began doubtfully. 'They've put a drawer in the back as a makeshift cot for the baby, and it's taken up most of the room.'

'Tara and I will travel in this one.' Before she had time to realise what was happening, Bryn steered Tara firmly into the passenger seat of a similar vehicle parked alongside, and Tara scowled. She had not reckoned on Bryn being invited, too. Paul must have asked him when she was walking with Meli to the vehicle park. If she had known, she would not have come. As it was, she would make sure her stay was a short one, she decided ungraciously. Overnight, in fact, and tomorrow morning she would throw herself on the mercy of the Consul, anything rather than be forced to endure Bryn's reluctant company for an hour longer than was absolutely necessary.

'Stay close,' Paul grinned across at them from the other vehicle, and Bryn replied, 'We will,' and got into the driving seat beside her. Tara's scowl deepened. She had reckoned on a soldier driving them, and now she was being denied even the relief of a third person in the vehicle. Fervently she hoped the journey would not be a long one. The two jeeps started off and rolled in convoy towards the high-gated entrance to the base, pausing at the junction with the public road. The first jeep peeled off to the right, going towards the town, and Bryn waited patiently while a large army transport vehicle full of soldiers pulled into the gates across their path.

'Paul told us to stay close,' Tara urged nervously. It would be the limit if they lost their way. In her present highly strung state she did not think she could cope with Bryn's sole company for any length of time, and she had no idea of the address of Paul's relatives if they should get parted.

'So he did,' Bryn agreed urbanely, and turned in the opposite direction.

'You're going the wrong way!' It took stunned seconds for his action to sink in, seconds while their vehicle picked up speed and increased the distance between the two jeeps. Tara glanced backwards, and already the other vehicle was almost out of sight. 'Where are you going?' she demanded furiously. 'Paul's driver turned to the right. Is this your idea of a joke?' she cried shrilly. It was not hers. Her sense of humour was not equal to being forcibly abducted twice within the space of a few days.

'We're going to Lamura. And it's no joke,' Bryn answered her questions in that order.

'For goodness' sake, stop fooling and turn the vehicle round, and follow Paul before we get hopelessly lost!' Tara shouted in exasperation. She was hopelessly lost already, wandering directionless in a deep blue mist from which there was no escape, but that was irremediable. This was not. 'Paul's relatives are expecting me,' she expostulated.

'On the contrary, even if they thought you were coming in the first place,' his lifted eyebrow correctly doubted that they did, 'Paul knows differently now.'

'You can't just carry me off against my will!' Tara rounded on him furiously. 'This is Hawaii, not Mahila. I'll shout for help to the military,' she threatened. The road still followed the perimeter fence of the military base, but she would have to be quick, she realised with dismay, because the fence, and the line of huts, was fast coming to an end.

'The soldiers would merely wave back and wish you a pleasant stay at Lamura,' Bryn assured her with insulting confidence, then his tone sharpened, defusing her continued protests. 'Remember that you're a foreign citizen on American soil. You're without a passport, or travel papers, or luggage.'

'I lost them all in the caravanette. You saw it washed out to sea,' Tara reminded him angrily.

'I saw the caravanette washed out to sea,' Bryn agreed calmly, 'but I didn't actually see any passport or travel papers in it, so I can't vouch. . . .'

'Don't split hairs!' Tara's patience snapped. 'Of course my passport and travel papers were in the vehicle,' she exploded, incensed by his cool analysis. 'It stands to sense. . . .'

'So it does,' Bryn nodded, 'but the authorities prefer proof.'

'How can I give them proof?' Tara demanded desperately. 'The only proof I've got is at the bottom of the sea, thanks to you,' she reminded him furiously. 'Until I can get to the British Consul and explain. . . .'

'Doubtless he'll provide all the proof you need,' Bryn allowed, 'and in the meantime I've agreed to stand surety for you—so long as you remain at Lamura,' he conditioned, and Tara's teeth ground at his impartial patronage.

'You've agreed to . . .? Oh no, this is too much!' she shouted angrily. 'Am I even allowed to ask what Lamura is? The local lock-up?' she hazarded sarcastically.

'On the contrary,' Bryn's lips twitched, 'Lamura's a very comfortable ranch house.'

'Yours?' Tara asked shortly.

'Mine,' he confirmed.

'In that case, my stay will be a one-night stand,' Tara assured him ungratefully. 'Tomorrow morning at first light, I'll be sitting on the steps of the Consulate, if I have to walk to get there!' She denied him the pleasure of refusing to drive her.

'You'll have to sit for a long time,' Bryn observed coolly.

'The doors open at nine o'clock.'

'Not this week,' he drawled, and Tara longed to hit him. 'It's a public holiday for three whole days.'

Three days of Bryn's company, under Bryn's roof. Was that what Paul meant when he said, 'Stay close?' The Hawaiian's humour was on par with Bryn's, Tara decided caustically, then went deathly still as another thought occurred to her.

Lamura was Bryn's ranch. Ergo, Roseanne would be at Lamura.

'How could you?' she gasped.

'How could I what?' His look was blank.

'Drag me to your home looking like this.' She indicated her dishevelled condition with a despairing sweep of her hand. 'Take me back to the military base this instant,' she demanded. 'I'm scratched, filthy from head to foot, and as if that isn't enough, you tore my skirt from hem to pocket.'

'If you go round saying things like that, people will think the very worst,' he mocked her, and carried on driving. 'In any case, apart from the torn skirt, I'm in the same state as you are.'

'It's all right for you, you're going home. I'm going to. . . .' She nearly said, 'to meet Roseanne.' She stopped herself just in time. If she absolutely *had* to meet Roseanne, she would prefer it to be on her own terms, becomingly dressed, and wearing high-heeled shoes to boost her confidence.

'You're coming to Lamura as my guest,' Bryn finished for her firmly. 'And once there, we can find you a change of clothes.'

Roseanne's clothes? The prospect was repugnant, but because she had lost her travel documents, as well as everything she stood up in, she must somehow endure it for the next three days.

She sat hunched in mutinous silence as the jeep hummed busily on, climbing steadily all the time. Signs of cultivation began to take over from the jungle, and patches of pineapple and fields of sugar cane slid past them as their wheels spun swiftly along the red earth roads, leading always upwards. After some miles of this the road surface deteriorated, and Bryn slowed the vehicle to a more moderate pace as the cultivation gave way to rich, waving grassland, on which herds of Hereford cattle grazed, their glossy coats nearly matching the dirt road for colour. As a concession to the ever-increasing potholes, Bryn slowed the jeep still further, and his eyes became keen on the cattle as they passed, while Tara leaned back in her seat and let the sunshine play on her face. A lark rose from the grass to one side of them, trilling into the blue dome overhead, and she watched its ascent absently. Apart from the plume of smoke on the distant horizon, that made a dark reminder of Mahila, it might have been high summer in England.

'Lamura's just ahead of us.'

The low, rambling ranch house, with its long, wide verandah, was a far cry from England. It was purely American in style, and a wide belt of trees sheltered it on the one side from the trade winds, giving it a cosy appearance in this high, upland valley. Bryn swung the jeep to a halt in front of the house, and a fair-haired woman rose from a lounger on the verandah and came towards them.

Roseanne?

Tara froze in her seat as she watched the newcomer approach. She was model-tall, and coolly elegant in pale green linen, with sandals to match. Her grooming was faultless, and from her appearance Tara judged her to be quite a lot older than Bryn. She reached the jeep at a leisurely pace, then leaned casually on the bonnet, waiting for Bryn to alight, and a wave of delicate perfume wafted to Tara on the warm air. It drove her fingers surreptitiously along her skirt, to make sure the pin she had borrowed from an amused soldier at the base was still doing its job of holding together the torn parts.

'I'll never forgive Bryn for bringing me here. Never!' she breathed. The contrast was devastatingly cruel, and Tara's embarrassment was complete—and it was all Bryn's fault, she blamed him bitterly. She remained in her seat and glowered as he swung himself from behind the wheel, and rounded the bonnet.

'Bryn, thank goodness you're safe!' The newcomer transferred her arms from the jeep bonnet and wound them round Bryn. 'When we heard the news bulletins on the wireless, we thought . . . we feared. . . .'

'I'm safe and sound, and so glad to see you.' Bryn leaned down and kissed her soundly on both cheeks, and Tara's glower turned to a puzzled frown. It was hardly the kind of salutation she expected him to give Roseanne.

'You look as if you could do with a bath and a good meal.' The fair-haired woman held him at arm's length and regarded him critically. 'I've got both ready for you in the house, but Con says you'll need a drink first. He's mixing one for you now.'

Con? Tara's bewilderment increased.

'Bless you, Liz, you've hit exactly the right note, as usual,' Bryn thanked her warmly.

Liz. Not Roseanne. Tara began to feel slightly lightheaded.

'Tara needs your ministrations even more than I do.' Bryn reached into the jeep and pulled Tara down beside him. 'The tidal wave took everything except what she stands up in.'

'Whose fault was that?' Tara's malevolent look asked him, but Bryn ignored it and continued smoothly, 'Tara, meet Liz.' Reluctantly she extended her hand and looked warily at the other woman, and was immediately disarmed by a pair of wide grey eyes, warmed by a friendly smile.

'I'll be able to kit you out,' Liz promised her readily, 'though I'm afraid my own clothes would swamp you, you're much too petite.' She made it sound like a sincere compliment, and Tara felt a rush of gratitude for her unexpected tact. She did not glance once at the torn skirt.

'Come along into the house, both of you, and have your drink first,' she urged, 'then we'll set about restoring you to normal.' She linked one arm in Bryn's and one in Tara's, walking in between them towards the verandah steps, and Tara found herself going along with them, her ego, if not yet restored to normal, at least considerably less dented than it was when she arrived. If her three days' stay at Lamura was all to be like this, with Liz to act as a buffer between herself and Bryn, then it might be just about bearable, Tara decided with rash optimism.

'Here are our refugees, Con,' Liz called out gaily as they entered the house. 'Come and meet my husband, Tara.' She ushered Tara into a long, low-ceilinged room that managed to combine comfort with grace in a way that spoke much for the taste and discrimination of her hostess.

'Welcome to Lamura.' Con was taller than his wife, and willow-thin, with a pleasant, rather ravaged-looking face, and Tara noticed with a quick flash of compassion, a distinct limp when he moved. His handshake was firm enough, however, and Tara accepted her glass with a sudden feeling of renewed confidence, that had been noticeably lacking since she first set eyes on Bryn.

'Now I'm going to sort out some clothes for you, while you wallow in a bath.' The introductions and the glass of wine finished, Liz showed Tara upstairs. 'Like I said, my own clothes will be too large for you,' she explained, 'but my daughter's gear should just about fit.' At one stroke she destroyed Tara's new-found confidence, and brought the tension back, and her heart hammered as she followed her hostess into a pretty bedroom.

'Your daughter?' She found it difficult to get the words out, but they had to be said, and she tensed as she waited for Liz's reply.

'Anne,' her mother enlarged. Doubtless short for Roseanne, Tara surmised bleakly, and felt a black cloud of depression settle on her shoulders as Liz went on brightly, 'She's away from home at the moment, but she'll be back with us again very soon.'

'Before that time comes, I'll be long gone from Lamura,' Tara vowed silently, and found slight comfort in her self-promise as she soaped and scrubbed in the adjoining bathroom, and thanked her lucky stars that she was blessed with naturally wavy hair that could be rubbed dry and left to its own devices when she donned her borrowed bathrobe, and returned to the room to find Liz surrounded by a welter of garments for all kinds of occasions.

'These are all new,' she explained. 'I got them ready for when Anne comes home. I thought you might prefer new ones, then you can take them with you afterwards. You'll need something to go on with until you can get your own wardrobe sorted out again.'

'I'll take them if you'll allow me to replace them later,' Tara stated firmly. She did not intend to place herself under any obligation to Bryn or any member of his household, for anything more than the three days' enforced stay at the ranch, and she pretended to examine the garments to hide the relief that she felt must surely show in her expression, that she would not, after all, need to wear clothes that had first been worn by Roseanne.

'Fine, if you want to, but there's no haste,' Liz insisted. 'You'll have to unstitch the labels, though.'

'Labels?' Tara picked up a pair of trews of the same bright colour as her own ill-used skirt, and frowned down at the label neatly sewn into the band at the back. It said,

'Anne Foster. Grade 5. Houston House.'

'Grade 5?' Tara looked her puzzlement at Liz.

'Anne goes up a grade when she returns to school in

the autumn,' he mother explained proudly. 'She'll be sixteen by then, but she takes after her father and me,' she admitted ruefully. 'She's a big girl for her age, and you're so tiny, her clothes are sure to fit.'

Not Roseanne, but Anne, aged only sixteen, and still at school! A laugh bubbled to Tara's lips, and she smiled across at Liz with what she hoped the other would think was delight in her offering.

'They're lovely.' She slid into the scarlet trews with genuine pleasure, and found them a perfect fit. So was the scarlet-and-white, gaily patterned top, and her spirits rose as she slipped it over her head and viewed her reflection in the mirror.

'It looks lovely,' Liz echoed the message of the mirror admiringly.

More to the point, it restored her confidence, Tara thought with satisfaction. The figure-hugging trews and top flattered her daintily curved form, and unconsciously she straightened. Clean, and properly dressed, she felt more than a match for Bryn now.

'Dinner.' Liz shooed her downstairs to where white linen and sparkling glass and cutlery covered the table in readiness. 'After a good meal, and a night's sleep, you'll feel on top the world.'

The world turned topsy-turvy, and her new-found confidence wavered and vanished when Tara looked across at Bryn. Both the men rose as they came into the room, and her heart gave a lurch as her eyes met Bryn's. The familiar white shirt and shorts had disappeared in favour of dark blue slacks that slimmed still further the already tight line of his hips, and a perfectly laundered silk shirt to match, that turned his eyes an even deeper blue. He looked every inch the master of Lamura, and, Tara caught a sharp breath, suddenly remote, and aloof, more of an enigma in his own background than he had been before. A cold feeling clutched at her, and Liz said,

'Tara, sit next to Bryn.' She would much rather have sat between Liz and Con, and eaten her meal in peace, but Bryn drew out her chair, and she sat down with an ill grace, feeling his hands touch her back with an electric contact that tingled down the length of her spine as he pushed her chair forward, closer to the table. Nervously she jinked away from his touch, and came into sharp contact with the table edge, and the water in her place glass slopped alarmingly close to a spill. She put out an urgent hand to steady it, wishing she could steady her own heartbeat as easily.

'Soup, missie?' An elderly Chinese in spotless whites padded to her side with a tempting-smelling tureen, and by the time he finished serving her and turned to do the same for Bryn, her breathing began to resume its normal pace, and the hot rich liquid helped her to cope with the disturbing awareness of him sitting next to her, eating alongside her, that she must somehow learn to come to terms with if she was to survive the next three days.

'It's nice to think you can salvage a few days of your holiday, even if you couldn't manage to rescue your belongings,' Con smiled at her across the table. 'It's a pity you chose this year to visit the area,' he added regretfully. 'The Pacific is the nearest thing I know to paradise, but this year it's gone out of its way to show its worst side. We don't usually have hurricanes, tidal waves and eruptions one after the other,' he excused his paradise. 'This year, it's been a savage summer. The islands have taken a beating.'

'Not only the islands,' Tara added a bleak, silent rider, but aloud she merely commented,

'The loss of my passport is the biggest nuisance.' It tied her to Bryn, obliging her to accept his hospitality, and for a few days at least put her at the mercy of his whims. She could not bring herself to regard the next three days as a holiday. From where she sat, they

appeared more of a test of endurance that, given
Bryn's close proximity, she felt less than equal to.

'You'll be able to remedy that easily enough after
the public holiday's over,' Liz consoled her.

'The salvaging of your yacht won't be so easy to
deal with,' Con put in. 'Do you think the *Gull* can be
raised and made seaworthy again?' he asked Bryn.

'I wasn't using my own yacht,' Bryn answered
calmly, and Tara went tense inside at his words. Not
using his own yacht? Then whose? Her breathing
seemed to stop as he forked food into his mouth, and
chewed for what seemed an interminable time before
he continued casually, 'The *Gull*'s in dock for an
engine refit. One of the main bearings has been giving
trouble recently, and I didn't want to risk taking her
out of home waters in that condition, so I hired the
Roseanne from the boatyard rather than postpone my
fishing trip. She was a pleasant enough vessel, but she
didn't handle as well as the *Gull*,' he added with an
owner's pride. 'And now, of course. . . .' He shrugged
significantly.

The *Roseanne* was a hired boat, it did not belong to
Bryn. Its name was just that, a name, and nothing
more. Nothing whatever to Bryn. Tara ate the rest of
her dinner with her mind in a daze, and Liz spoke to
her three times before the waiting silence at the table
warned her that she was expected to offer something
in answer.

'I'm sorry, I didn't quite catch. . . .' she began
confusedly.

'We should be the ones to apologise, for keeping you
up,' Liz said remorsefully. 'Off to bed with you, and
sleep the clock round. We can show you the ranch
tomorrow, when you're rested. I'll take you to your
room.'

'I'll take her, and go up myself as well.' Bryn
pushed his chair back and waited for Tara to rise.

'I'll find my own way,' she asserted independently the moment the room door closed behind them.

'Since I'm accountable for your welfare for the next few days,' Bryn returned smoothly, 'I must make sure you don't get lost.'

'Or don't try to escape?' Tara flashed, and seized her opportunity while it presented itself. 'I'm not all you're accountable for,' she reminded him forcefully. 'There's the matter of the caravanette to be settled.'

'The van will be insured by the hiring company, the same as the *Roseanne*,' Bryn replied indifferently, and Tara's indignation spilled over.

'You won't get away with it so easily as that,' she vowed, 'I won't let you. It's entirely your fault that the van was lost. I parked it on the windward side of Mahila, where it would have been safe. You were responsible for bringing it on to the leeward side, *against my will*,' she reminded him wrathfully. 'It was the leeward side of the island which caught the full force of the tidal wave.'

'So?' Bryn shrugged. 'The van was destroyed by the tidal wave.' His voice changed and hardened, and he continued deliberately, 'Destroyed a mere twenty-four hours before it would have been just as surely destroyed by the lava flow that came down on the windward side of the island. It's been a savage summer, remember?' he used Con's words to mock her.

His kiss was savage. It was as fierce as the hurricane; as overwhelming as the tidal wave; and it burned hotter than the heat from the volcano. It drove her lips back against her teeth, and her protest back into her protesting throat. It punished her for her temerity in daring to lay the blame on him, and showed no mercy on her tiredness. Tara fought him with beating fists, and her last reserves of strength, but he was too strong for her, and his lips had their way with her own until they were bruised and breathless, and her strength was spent. Her fists grew heavy and ceased their frantic beating against his chest, and she felt her senses begin to slip. With a low moan she went limp, and her last conscious impression as she slipped into oblivion was of Bryn's arms catching her, lifting her up, and the firm tread of his feet as he began slowly to ascend the stairs.

CHAPTER NINE

THE clink of a spoon against china roused her, and Tara stirred and opened her eyes. Bright sunshine streamed through the open window, and from somewhere a clock chimed the hour of ten. She counted the strokes drowsily, one, two, three. By the tenth she was wide awake, and she looked round her curiously. She was lying on a narrow guest bed, in a cheerfully furnished room not unlike the one in which Liz had produced the selection of clothes the night before. The night before. . . .

Memory flooded back, and she pushed the sheet away and struggled upright, then looked down at herself in sheer consternation. When Bryn had carried her up to bed the night before she was dressed in scarlet trews and a scarlet-and-white patterned top. Now—she swallowed consulsively—the trews and top rested neatly across tve back of a nearby chair, and she was encased in a dainty, off-the-shoulder shortie nightdress that revealed almost as much as it covered.

'Awake at last?' The room door opened, and Liz greeted her cheerfully. 'I've brought you some breakfast, so that you can get up when you feel like it. How *do* you feel this morning?' She sat companionably on the end of the bed and scanned Tara's face with alert eyes.

'I'm fine,' Tara discovered, and viewed with relish the daintily laid tray that Liz laid on her lap.

'You weren't last night,' her hostess said candidly, and nodded her satisfaction at her guest's appetite as Tara started hungrily on the contents of the tray. 'You passed out in the hall on your way upstairs, and Bryn carried you to bed.'

'I don't remember,' Tara lied, and felt her cheeks burn at the memory. She looked appealingly across at Liz. 'How . . . who . . .?' She stammered to a halt, and her embarrassed look begged an answer from the older woman to the question she could not bring herself to frame.

'Don't worry—I undressed you, with Mary's help. She's our housekeeper.' Liz defined her fears and set them at rest with a merry look. 'Fortunately Bryn caught you in his arms before you fell, and he kicked open the dining room door and shouted for me to help him,' she twinkled.

Bryn's had not been the hands that ministered to her. He had shouted for help, carried her to bed, then left her to the attentions of Liz and the unknown Mary. Tara finished her breakfast on a wave of relief, liberally mixed with an acute sense of loss. Ruthlessly she subdued the loss. Bryn had evidently not thought fit to explain to Liz the reason *why* she had passed out the night before, she realised caustically, and wondered what her hostess would say if she told her. With an effort she resisted the impulse to expose Bryn. If she did, it was doubtful if Liz would believe her, she and Con seemed to be besotted by Bryn, she thought cynically, and wondered what was their position at Lamura. There was no recognisable likeness between the three, which ruled out their being members of Bryn's family. She finished the last of her coffee thoughtfully. On his own admission, the ranch belonged to Bryn. That fitted in nicely with his description of himself as 'a sort of cowhand'. But. . . . His remark last night about the *Gull* returned to tease her.

'I don't want to risk taking her out of home waters,' he said. Surely if he owned Lamura, the surrounding

Pacific should be 'home waters' to him? Another question to add to the seemingly endless list of questions about Bryn. Tara sighed. The moment one question was answered, another one rose to take its place.

'I'll leave you to get dressed now,' Liz interrupted her train of thought, and removed the empty tray as she made her way to the door. 'As soon as you're ready, come downstairs and join us. You'll be able to see something of the ranch today, there's a colt in the top pastures that Con wants Bryn to look at.'

The outing would be just about bearable with Liz and Con as referees, Tara decided. She dreaded meeting Bryn again. He had given no explanation to Liz last night of why she collapsed, but would he remain silent when she came face to face with him this morning? The uncertainty was a torment that dragged her feet to a halt on the outside of the room door downstairs.

'They're all on the verandah, Miss Brodie. Go straight through,' an elderly woman whose white hair and comfortable proportions proclaimed her to be the housekeeper smiled at Tara cross the hall.

'Thank you, Mary.' Tara hoped her own answering smile disguised her quickened heartbeat as she turned the knob and nerved herself to cross the empty room towards the outer door, through which she could hear voices engaged in desultory conversation.

'It's a lovely glossy chestnut, with a white blaze.' Con's voice, describing the colt. He was lying back on a swinging hammock, with a scatter of newspapers and periodicals on the cushions beside him, and Liz lay in the lounger leafing through a glossy magazine. Bryn leaned with his back against the verandah rail, and he looked up as Tara appeared through the door. The sun was behind him, and it shone in her eyes and curtained his face with a dark shadow. The dazzle prevented her from drawing aside the curtain and, frustrated, she screwed up her eyes and used the sun as an excuse to turn aside and say to Liz, in a voice that held a slight quaver,

'I hope I haven't kept you waiting?'

She felt no regret at making Bryn wait, but she had nothing against Liz or Con, and the niceties had to be observed.

'There's no haste,' Liz assured her lazily. 'It's a beautiful morning for the trip.'

'I'm looking forward to it,' Tara assured her, and meant it. With fresh scenery to divert her mind, and Liz and Con for company, it would pass the day safely, and then there was only the evening to get through. Anything was better than the risk of being alone with Bryn.

'Now you're here. . . .' Bryn pushed himself off the verandah rail and made as if to take her by the arm, and Tara sidestepped hastily. She would be lost if he touched her again. To avoid the risk she ran ahead of him to the waiting jeep, but hesitated uncertainly when she saw a bulky box taking up most of the back seat.

'Sit in the front,' Bryn told her.

'I'll sit in the back with Liz.' Her looked levelled with his, and defied him.

'We're not coming with you,' Liz announced regretfully from the verandah above them. 'Anne said she'd ring us from school some time today, to tell us how she got on in her end-of-term exams, but she didn't say what time she'd make the call.'

'Our daughter's a scatterbrain, but we must be in when she rings.' Con's smile said he did not mind the sacrifice.

'We'll see you both at dinner,' Liz added. 'Have a nice day.'

Dinner. A whole day, spent in Bryn's sole company.

Certainly not a nice one, Tara predicted unhappily. She racked her brains to find a valid excuse to remain at the house, but none presented itself. Unwisely, she had told Liz she felt fine. Her hostess had watched her demolish her breakfast with a hearty appetite, and she had just said she was looking forward to the trip. And consideration demanded she must not make an unwanted third in the house when Liz and Con took their daughter's call, and sat down together afterwards to discuss her news.

'Sit in the front,' Bryn repeated, and this time there was a ring of steel in his voice.

She sat in the front. Wrathfully, reluctantly, ignoring his proffered helping hand, she clambered into the front passenger seat, uncomfortably aware of Liz and Con leaning over the verandah rail above her, able to see her every movement. If she defied Bryn and sat in the back seat, they would wonder what on earth she was doing. There would be comment, and questions. Rather than face them she capitulated, and sat humped in the seat, hoping ill-temperedly that the vehicle would refuse to start.

The engine fired first time, and Tara returned the couple's waves as the jeep started off smoothly, feeling as if she was being cut off from her only security. The sun was warm, and the breeze bent the long-stemmed grasses into moving waves in the pasture land on either side of the red dirt road, making the ruddy-coated cattle appear as if they were standing in a moving sea. A hawk hovered motionless on the air currents above them, casting the pastures for some movement that would indicate food, and Tara shivered, suddenly cold. She became aware of the jeep slowing down, and lowered her gaze from the sky, then went colder still as her horrified gaze met that of an immense Hereford bull, standing directly in the path of the jeep and regarding her through the windscreen with bovine curiosity.

'Keep going, for goodness' sake!' her voice rose in a frightened squeak, and she shrank against Bryn's side as the huge head wagged from side to side. 'Keep going!'

'He's peaceful enough,' Bryn laughed. 'He's got more important matters on his mind than chasing us,' he grinned, and stood up in his seat and leaned over the windscreen and waved his arms at the animal with a sharp, 'Giddup!' and Tara breathed a sigh of relief as the bull snorted, and lumbered off into the grassland after its harem of cows.

'More important . . .? Oh!' She felt her cheeks grow hot, and Bryn's grin grew wider. She put up her hand to shield her face, and knew confusedly that she was too late. Bryn's sidelong glance mocked her rising colour, and she gritted her teeth at his amused chuckle. Then, without warning, she found herself laughing with him, and the sunshine and the high upland pastures took on a magic quality, that spilled over and silvered the rest of the untouched day.

Bless Liz and Con for stopping at home! Bless the Hereford bull for stopping in front of them! The hawk drifted away on the wind, and a skylark rose trilling in its place, and her spirits rose to match. Bryn set the jeep in motion again, speeding smoothly along the dirt road until it widened into a four-way junction. He slowed, and swung to the right, and the bonnet began to dip steeply downhill in front of them.

'Surely Con said the colt was in the top pasture? Shouldn't that be uphill, not down?' Tara sat upright and viewed the changing terrain with a frown. The grassland slid behind them and the first signs of cultivation began to appear, reversing the order of their journey the day before. Sugar cane grew tall beside the road.

'There's no haste, we've got all day,' Bryn answered her easily. 'While we're out, you may as well see something of the island. The parts the touring coaches never reach,' he teased.

'Our coaches reach most places, and we do most things,' Tara defended her firm's itineraries with quick pride.

'Have you ever tasted raw sugar, straight from the cane?' he challenged.

'No-o,' she was forced to admit.

'Try some now, it's an experience not to be missed. It's like no sugar you've ever tasted before.' He braked to a halt beside the tall canes and rummaged in the back of the vehicle, to come up with something that to Tara looked to be a cross between a knife and a chopper. Carefully selecting a cane, he bent down, and with an ease that told her it was not the first time he had done it, he severed the cane at the base with one sharp chop.

'It's the local children's equivalent of a stick of rock,' he smiled, and cut off two handy sized pieces, throwing the rest in the back of the jeep.

'Surely it's too hard to eat?' Tara looked at the cane doubtfully.

'You don't eat the cane, you peel off the outer coating, like this,' he wielded the knife expertly, and in a moment had one of the pieces of cane stripped of its outer layer. 'Now chew on the inner fibres to make them release their juice,' he handed it to her, and added, 'when it's drained of its sweetness, just throw the fibres away.'

It was an apt description of the way he had treated her heart, she thought bitterly. His kisses had drained it of its sweetness until only the dried husk remained. He had taken the joy, and callously discarded the rest, leaving behind only the ache for her. But the free-running sap of the sugar cane sweetened the bitterness, and the sun acted as a balm to the ache, and she chewed at the tough fibres until all the sweetness was gone, then licked her fingers free of the juice and asked with unassumed interest,

'Where now?'

'There's a small orchid farm nearby. I thought you might be interested.' Bryn tossed away the remains of his own cane and slid behind the wheel of the jeep.

'An orchid farm? I didn't know.'

'You didn't know, and you a courier?' he mocked, but it was friendly raillery, with no sting behind it, and Tara swung out of the jeep beside him and followed him willingly enough towards a row of what looked like packing sheds, a few miles further along the road.

'A lot of the crop from here is exported.' Bryn seemed to know the place well, and guided her with the confidence of familiarity.

''Morning, Mr Mathieson. Hello, Bryn.'

Greetings were called to him from all sides, and another question began to form at the back of Tara's mind.

'Come and see the orchids.' Before it had time to take shape, Bryn drew her into the largest of the sheds. Outside, it was a modest enough structure, as unpretentious as a barn. Inside, it glowed with vivid colour. It was as if a flock of brilliant butterflies had settled on the benches, and Tara gasped at the endless variety of colour and form in the perfect blooms. She wandered between the benches, lost in wonder at the display, watching each orchid skilfully packed to protect it on its forthcoming plane journey to destinations as exotic as the blooms themselves. She wondered who would wear the long, arching spray of pale green blossoms, or the large, single purple flower, that was surely meant to grace a bosom of impressive proportions, she decided with a smile.

'A prima donna, no less.' Bryn's voice was low and amused in her ear, latching on to her thoughts with

uncanny ease, and they laughed together, happy,
shared laughter, savouring the joke between them. He
reached down and caught her hand, and she did not
try to pull away, and linked together they wandered
through the rest of the sheds until they both felt they
had had a surfeit of orchids.

'Choose one before we leave.' He drew her to a final
table of ready packed boxes, the transparent lids
revealing a bewildering variety from which to make
her choice.

'I don't know . . .' Tara hesitated over first one, and
then another, and finally picked up a box near the
edge of the table, her eye caught by the rich brown-
and-cream candy-striping of the large, exotic bloom
inside. It was crisply fresh, and exquisitely beautiful,
but . . .

'That one's not for you.' Bryn took it from her hand
and put it back in its place on the table, and picked up
another box instead. 'This is your bloom,' he said, and
pressed it into her hand as he led her away from the
bench and back into the sunshine to the jeep.

'How typical of you!' Tara exploded, all her
pleasure in the flower vanished in a rush of
indignation at his high-handed action. She tossed the
box he had given to her into the front of the jeep
without bothering to glance at its contents. 'You offer
me the pick of the blooms, and as soon as I've chosen
one I like, you immediately take it from me and
substitute one of your own choosing instead. How
typically   arrogant   of   you!'   she   stormed.
Disappointment and temper corroded her tongue, and
she lashed out regardless, wanting to hurt.

'The bloom you chose didn't suit you.'

'And yours does, I suppose?' she asked sarcastically.

'Yes.'

Just that. No hint that he might be mistaken. No
concession to her own opinion. Just, yes. Full stop.

Tara choked on the uncompromising surety of it. The engine started and covered her choke, and Bryn added casually as they pulled away from the packing sheds,

'When you look at it, you'll see I'm right.'

She refused to look at it. She refused to give Bryn the satisfaction of showing any interest whatever in his gift. She sat in a tight silence as he drove back uphill along the road by which they had come, past the sugar cane plantation, back among the pastureland to the four-way junction, where he turned on to the main track and continued uphill.

'The top pasture's just ahead.' Unlike the others Tara saw it was fenced, and instead of cattle, her eyes picked out a small herd of some twenty or more thoroughbred horses.

'There don't seem to be many here, for a ranch,' she criticised.

'The ranch runs cattle. The horses are Con's hobby.'

That answered one question, at least. She asked another. 'Where's the colt?'

'Over there, by the far fence.' Bryn pointed, and Tara saw a flash of chestnut among a group of young animals that were venting their high spirits by racing each other round the perimeter fence.

'Let's take our lunch on to the grass and watch him,' Bryn suggested. 'I want to see how he moves.'

The grass was soft and thick, and sweetly scented, ideal for grazing, perfect as a cushion for a picnic. Bryn brought the box from the back of the jeep and lifted out a flask, and the sharp aroma of coffee, as good as only Americans can make it, wafted temptingly on the warm air. He produced new, yeasty rolls and sharp crumbling cheese, that made a banquet with the inevitable fresh pineapple, and they topped it by generous slices of rich, home-made fruit cake, and finished off with small rusty-skinned oranges similar to the one they had eaten on Mahila. Tara took one, and her eyes sought Bryn's across the picnic box. On Mahila they had shared her orange. Would he remember? Would he want to do the same with this one? She scanned his features hopefully for some sign that he remembered, some glance of recognition that this was something they had shared together, but she looked in vain. Bryn's eyes were fixed on the galloping colt, his fingers peeling his orange with absent movements that told Tara his mind was not on his task, not remembering.

A feeling of flatness invaded her. The orange was sharp, and the juice bit at her tongue and soured the tasty meal she had just eaten. She put the other half of the fruit, the half Bryn should have shared with her, back into the box, then got up restlessly and wandered to the fence, staring moodily across at the horses while Bryn put the picnic box back into the jeep. When he joined her at the fence, he had a rope looped in his right hand.

'I want a closer look at the colt,' he answered her enquiring look.

'You mean you're going to lasso him?' She had seen it done on films, but had not expected to witness it in real life.

'How else?' He climbed on to the fence and vaulted down on to the grass on the other side. 'At the pace he's running now, he'll be close enough to rope within a minute or two. You stay where you are, on the other side of the fence,' he cautioned Tara, 'just in case the colt gets rough.'

'You won't hurt him?' She made it plain her sympathies were with the colt.

'I won't hurt him, so long as he comes quietly.'

'And if he doesn't?' she flashed. 'What then?' she insisted hotly.

'He's got to learn not to fight the rope,' Bryn stated

flatly. 'By the time he's pulled it tight once or twice, he'll soon discover that it's policy not to back away. Now be quiet,' he ordered her peremptorily, 'he's coming close.'

If the colt backed away, the noose round its neck would pull tight, and . . . Tara caught a painful breath. Bryn stood tensed and waiting, the rope curled ready in his hands. The colt raced closer, outdistancing its fellows, a young, strong, proud creature, glorying in its freedom. As yet, Tara realised, it had not noticed the waiting man. The sun glinted on the rich chestnut coat, on the black tossing mane and the proudly arched neck, round which the rope would drop, and pull tight. Bryn swung the loop round his head, once, twice, three times, and threw.

'No!' Tara exploded into action. She could not allow the colt to run blindly into the lasso, into captivity. She knew just what it felt like to be captured by Bryn, the frantic desire to be free, and the hopeless, choking inevitability of no escape. She could not allow it to happen to the colt. 'Go away. Shoo! Giddup!' She scrambled on to the top of the fence and shouted at the top of her voice, unconsciously using Bryn's own phraseology as she waved both arms violently above her head.

The effect of her sudden appearance was all she could desire. The colt gave a startled whinny and reared violently, curvetting to one side on its rear hooves.

'— — —!' The rope fell short. Another second, and the loop would have circled the colt's neck. Instead, it lay limp and useless on the grass, and with a shrill neigh its intended victim came down on all fours, then bolted off at a tangent towards the other side of the pasture, followed in a bunch by the rest of its fellows.

'What on earth possessed you to do that?' Bryn swung to confront her across the fence. His face was livid with fury, and Tara felt a quick thrill of fear at

the expression in his eyes. He pulled in the slack rope
with quick, angry jerks, and looped it back in his
hand. 'Now the animal's been alarmed, it'll be wary,
and twice as difficult to catch,' he shouted at her
angrily.

'Then let it go free.' Tara backed away warily as he
strode closer to the other side of the fence.

'Horses aren't bred to be set free, they have to earn
their living, the same as human beings,' Bryn retorted,
and glared at her across the wooden poles. 'Go and sit
in the jeep out of the way,' he snarled. 'Thanks to you
I might be ages roping the colt now!'

'Take all the time you want, and then some,' Tara
taunted with a sudden upsurge of courage. A plan
flashed fully formed into her mind, beautiful in its
simplicity, so that she wondered why she had not
thought of it before. 'By the time you've walked back to
the ranch house, I'll be with Paul and Meli in town, and
you can keep your ranch, and your horse, and your
orchid. You're cruel and heartless!' Tears threatened to
choke her, and she spun round and took to her heels
before they spilled over, and fled towards the jeep. Bryn
had left the ignition key in the lock, she had only to
jump into the driving seat, turn the key and debrake,
and she would be away before Bryn had time to climb
the fence. The moment she was beyond his reach she
would jettison his orchid, and he could have it to
console him on his long walk back to Lamura.

She was within a foot of the vehicle when the rope
dropped round her shoulders. A faint swishing sound
was all the warning she received. She heard it, and
looked up, startled, and seconds passed before she
realised her peril, and by then it was too late.
Frantically she tried to grasp the rope and lift it from
off her, but before she could curl her fingers round the
hempen strands the loop pulled tight, pinioning her
arms to her sides.

'Take this thing off me!' She struggled ineffectually to free herself as Bryn strolled unhurriedly towards her, keeping the rope tight between them, and pulling it in hand over hand as he advanced, bearing down on her like a male Nemesis, intent on extracting vengeance for her rash act.

'Loose me this instant,' she panted furiously. 'I'm supposed to be your guest, not a prisoner of war!' She was a prisoner of the never-ending war between man and woman, and she turned at bay, with the light of battle firing the tiny gold flecks in her eyes as Bryn reached her, and substituted his hands for the rope.

'I'll make you pay for what you did,' he promised her harshly, and with cold deliberation he pulled her to him and took his time to extract the last ounce of payment from her quivering lips. The rope was rough against her bare arms, rubbing a raw weal on her soft flesh. The grip of his fingers was mercilessly tight, making the rope seem kind by comparison. He pressed her against him, his lean frame hard and unyielding, and she felt fury shiver through him like a living current, ready to burn and destroy. She stared up into his face with dilated eyes, and he closed her lids with angry lips. With every ounce of her strength she strained away from him, and the rope fell unheeded round her feet as she twisted her face from side to side to try to escape his kisses, until he cupped his hand round the back of her head and forced her into stillness. She could no longer move. She could no longer breathe. The hard, angry blue of his eyes swam in her vision. Despairingly she knew she must submit, as inevitably the colt would have to submit, because she had no strength left with which to fight him any longer.

'Don't try to escape me, Tara.'

In her present state she was incapable of trying to escape, just as she was incapable of resistance when he lifted her up and put her in the passenger seat of the jeep, then pulled the key from the ignition and put it safely out of her reach in his pocket.

'*You* can walk back to Lamura, if you want to,' he growled, 'I'm going to rope the colt.'

With anguished eyes she watched him stalk the colt, using as cover the mature, less easily panicked horses grazing in the middle of the paddock. They continued placidly nose to the grass while Bryn set the young stock in motion again, trotting uneasily back round the perimeter fence. The colt was almost opposite to the jeep, keeping close to the rails, when Bryn appeared from the midst of the grazing mares and swung his lasso. Had he deliberately waited, Tara wondered dully, until the young animal was close to where she sat, so that she should witness its subjugation? She could not prove that he had, she could only suspect, and hate Bryn for what she suspected.

She did not want to look, but her eyes glued themselves to the scene in front of her with a fearful fascination, and she could not tear them away. Bryn swung the rope and the loop sailed through the air, and Tara winced as her ears caught its familiar, sinister *swish*. The colt heard it too, and jerked up its head, which was exactly what Bryn intended it should do, and the loop settled neatly over its head and drew tight round the glossy chestnut neck.

Immediately it felt the rope the colt began to fight to get free. It lunged and kicked and reared, and Tara felt sick. It was like watching a replay of her own battle with Bryn, knowing that the colt, like herself, would inevitably lose. Bryn advanced on the animal, keeping the rope tight between them, pulling it in hand-over-hand exactly as he had done with herself, only this time with a difference. This time he talked as he walked forward, speaking in a low, coaxing voice to the frightened colt. The animal responded with nervous head tossings and continued to back away, still fighting the rope, until its rump came up hard against the sturdy wooden bars behind it. Its eyes rolled, showing their whites, and repeatedly it reared high, its front hooves beating the air as it felt itself trapped between the unyielding fence and the inexorably advancing man, and a thrill of apprehension ran through Tara as she watched.

'Bryn, be careful!'

She did not realise she had cried out loud. She did not know if Bryn had heard her. She was only conscious of the pawing hooves, and Bryn's bare head, his hair glinting in the sunlight. She clutched the back of the seat, and the knuckles of her fingers showed white as she strained forward to watch, dreading to see the flailing hooves strike him to the ground.

'Bryn, don't go any nearer,' she begged urgently.

For all the notice he took of her, she might as well have saved her breath. She watched fearfully as he continued to walk, purposefully, unhesitatingly, towards the rearing colt.

'Bryn, oh, Bryn . . .' His name was wrenched from her lips in a tortured plea.

'Whoa there, my beauty. Whoa!' Still talking, still walking, still pulling the rope tight between them, Bryn approached closer, and the rope became shorter, bringing the colt's head down, and its hooves along with it, until the animal stood on all four feet, snorting and quivering while Bryn's hand ran reassuringly along its neck, patting, soothing, gentling the creature to the feel of his touch, and the sound of his voice. There was a mesmeric quality about his performance, and after a while the colt ceased its snorting and head tossing, and though it still quivered, it stood more or less quietly under Bryn's hand, and Tara leaned back limply in her seat, her reaction swift anger against him for the fright he had given her.

'If he thinks he can quieten me so easily, he's in for a shock,' she vowed irefully. 'He'll discover I'm made of sterner stuff than the colt!'

For a time Bryn continued to talk and stroke, and then, when he was satisfied with the colt's response, he quietly slipped the noose free from the animal's neck, and stepped back. For an electric second the creature remained still, and Tara held her breath, then the colt realised it was free, and with a shrill whinny and a flurry of hooves it was gone, racing round Bryn and away, to the other side of the pasture, as far away from its captor as the perimeter fence would allow. Bryn remained for a moment, watching it gallop away, then he turned and vaulted the fence and rejoined Tara at the jeep, and she tensed as he got into the driving seat beside her.

'That's enough—for today.' There was no mistaking his double meaning, or the look he turned on her, and Tara jerked her chin up sharply and met the challenge in his eyes with a defiant stare, but before she could speak he went on, 'The colt will be harder to catch the next time,' he inclined his head towards the paddock. 'Now he's had a taste of captivity, he'll keep as far away as he can when he sees me again.'

'I know just how he feels,' Tara retorted spiritedly, and longed to strike him as Bryn laughed, a low, amused, supremely confident laugh that lilted in his voice as he answered,

'Never fear, he'll come to hand eventually. It's only a matter of time.'

'With the colt, maybe,' she flashed back, her fierce independence rising at his cool assurance that, she felt convinced, included herself as well as the colt. 'With the colt, but not with me,' she declared with a toss of her head that unconsciously identified with the recent captive. 'Never, ever, with me!' she asserted proudly.

CHAPTER TEN

'HAVE you enjoyed your day?'

'What did you think of the colt? Did you manage to get a close look at him?'

Liz and Con strolled down the verandah steps to greet them, and Tara ejected from her seat in the jeep with the exuberance of relief the moment Bryn braked to a halt. Another minute of the brittle silence in which they had just completed their journey, and she would have screamed, she decided raggedly.

'It's been a lovely day,' she prevaricated. The weather had been perfect. Not so the day. She refused to perjure herself by pretending she had enjoyed the day. Her reply seemed to satisfy Liz, and Bryn could make what he pleased of it, she told herself defensively.

'Tara.' He spoke from behind her, like the voice of conscience, and she spun round, startled. She had expected him to be on the other side of the jeep. Instead he climbed across the seat and descended from the vehicle on the same side as herself, and when she turned he was right beside her, and the flower box was in his hand.

'You've forgotten your orchid.'

With impeccable timing he held it out towards her just as Liz and Con came up to them, and there was nothing she could do but hold out her hand and take it from him. It was impossible to make a scene in front of the others, and Bryn knew it, and used the knowledge ruthlessly to force her to accept his rejected gift. Tara's look was venomous as he pressed the box into her hand and curled her fingers round it, forcing

her to hold it. She winced as a corner of the box dug
into her palm, but the pressure of his hand over her
own did not relax until her gasped, 'Thank you,'
released her. Furiously she massaged the reddened
dint on her palm where the box had dug in, and
longed, but did not quite dare, in front of Bryn, to tell
Liz she could have the hated flower to keep for herself
when her hostess exclaimed,

'What a gorgeous orchid! Aren't the colours
beautiful?'

Tara did not know what the colours were.
Deliberately she had kept her eyes averted from the
flower, and despised herself for the irresistible
curiosity that made her look at it now.

The packaging of the bloom was not unlike the
barrier which Bryn put round himself, she compared
them bitterly. It was transparent, almost invisible, but
strong enough to withstand any attempt to break
through. She felt bruised and battered by her hopeless
attempts to break through, and the flower did nothing
to console her for her failure. She stared fixedly down
at it for tense seconds before the colours registered on
her resisting mind.

'This is your bloom,' he had said. The bloom which
Bryn decided best suited her. Was this how he saw her?
A stifled feeling stole her breath, and a shiver started
in the fingers that held the transparent box, and
trembled right through her as she took in the delicate
beauty of the orchid in her hand. It was small, and
exquisitely formed, with petals of a warm cream, tipped
with vivid gold, borrowing fire from the deep, rich heart
of the bloom that glowed like a living flame in her
suddenly shaking hand. Was this how Bryn saw her?

She tore her eyes away from the orchid and fixed
them on his face, searching for an answer, but his
expression was closed against her, and if he noticed
her appealing look he gave no sign, but spoke to Con

in answer to his question as they walked all together up the verandah steps.

'I managed to rope the colt, and handle him for a few minutes.' Tara held her breath. Would he say anything about her own part in the roping? Perhaps laugh with Con and Liz at the way he had roped her? She gritted her teeth at the searing humiliation of it, and longed to take to her heels and run to her room and hide her shame as Bryn went on easily, 'It took two attempts, but the second one was successful, and he calmed down very well after a while.' He said nothing about her own part in the roping, nothing about roping her, and Tara let out her breath in a tiny puff of relief, although she felt no gratitude to Bryn for his discretion as he continued to Con, 'I'll go up to the top paddock each day from now on, and by the time I leave he should have gentled down sufficiently to be ready to ship home. It'll take about a month, I reckon.'

'These two will talk about horses all the evening.' Liz took Tara by the arm. 'Let's leave them to it, and go upstairs and change for dinner. Will you wear your orchid?' she asked, coming into Tara's bedroom some time later. 'It'll go nicely with that cream dress.'

'I don't think. . . .' Tara began. She did not want to wear the orchid. It disturbed her, as did the questions it posed in her mind, still more questions about Bryn, and she did not want it on her shoulder as an uncomfortable reminder of its donor, who disturbed her even more. 'I thought I'd leave it in my room, in a glass of water,' she hedged lamely.

'Oh, do wear it,' Liz pressed her. 'You can always put it in water afterwards. It'll turn the dinner into an occasion,' she coaxed. 'We can celebrate Anne's exam results.'

'They're good ones, then?' Tara grasped at the exam results to turn the conversation away from the orchid.

'Very good,' Liz confirmed proudly. 'Anne's done extremely well. We'll tell you all about it later. It'll make a pleasant change from listening to talk about horses,' she sighed resignedly. 'We'll have the colt's pros and cons for breakfast, lunch and dinner, every day now until Bryn ships the animal home,' she predicted ruefully.

'I thought Lamura was Bryn's home?' Tara said offhandedly. She sat in front of the dressing table mirror and fiddled with the orchid, placing it here and there against her dress as if she was trying to decide where it looked best, feigning indifference while her ears strained for Liz's reply, and every nerve of her willed her hostess to continue talking. An age seemed to pass before Liz said,

'Lamura belongs to Bryn, but Con manages it for him. Bryn lives on his home ranch, in Texas. He used to farm in England, but he settled in the States some years ago—his mother was American. I suspect he only bought Lamura to help Con,' she went on candidly. 'They'd known each other years back, and then Con was wounded in Vietnam. By the time he came out of hospital his firm had gone into liquidation, so his job was no longer there, and his confidence went when he couldn't get another one right away.' Her face clouded at the memory as she went on, 'We were really in the doldrums when Bryn found us. Apparently he'd been looking for Con for some time, but we'd moved to a smaller house downtown to cut down on expenses, and it took him a while to trace us. We'd got Anne by then, of course, and financially things were tight. Bryn came like the answer to a prayer,' she remembered gratefully.

'And you came to Lamura?' Tara encouraged her.

'Not right away. We went to Texas first, to the home ranch,' Liz continued obligingly. 'Con had a lot to learn about ranch management, and Bryn taught him all he knew. The original idea was that he should work on the home ranch, it's a huge outfit with more than enough room for someone else at the helm, but then oil was discovered on one part of it, and of course it immediately injected a lot of revenue into an already prosperous ranch, but typically, instead of spending it on himself, Bryn used it to buy Lamura and install Con in sole charge, which restored my husband's pride at the same time as the climate restored his health. He did the same for another man, with the orchid farm you went to today,' unwittingly she answered yet another question. 'I'll be grateful to Bryn for as long as I live,' Liz declared fervently. 'He comes over occasionally to visit us, and he and Con go marlin fishing together, but he never interferes with the running of the ranch, he leaves Con to manage it in his own way, as if it was his own spread.'

Which answered most of Tara's remaining questions, and added an entirely new dimension to her knowledge of Bryn. The insensitive, arrogant, dictatorial Bryn, who used his extra wealth to buy Lamura, in order to restore another man's pride.

The orchid burned a hole in her shoulder as she entered the dining room. Bryn's eyes fastened on the flower the moment she came through the door, and her hand rose nervously to touch the petals. She dragged it down again instantly, impatient with herself for betraying her nervousness, but Bryn's sharp glance saw the movement, and the gleam in his eye told her he recognised the reason for it. His eyes moved from the flower to her face, proving her heightened colour, and abruptly Tara turned aside and reached for her chair, not waiting for him to draw it out for her. She felt angry with herself for giving way to Liz and wearing the flower; angry with Bryn for insisting upon her taking it. Dinner seemed to drag on for ever, but at last it was over and she sat with the others on the verandah, and her ears listened while Liz and Con eulogised on their daughter's academic success, while her mind turned ceaselessly on what she had just learned about Bryn.

A gecko chuck-chucked on the verandah ceiling, and the soft call of wild doves made a peace of the evening as she mulled over this new and unexpected aspect of the man she had been with, and battled with, during the past few days, that encapsulated a lifetime of experience and still left him almost a complete stranger to her. She watched the sunset with brooding eyes, the colours less vivid because she sat beside Liz to watch it, while Bryn leaned beside Con on the verandah rail.

'The eruption on Mahila seems to be dying down at last,' Con remarked lazily, anent the thin spiral of smoke on the far horizon, that now took the place of the fiery display which rivalled the sunset on the previous evening.

'That'll make Mary happy,' Liz chuckled. 'She's been complaining all day about the cinder dust. Even at this distance it's covered all the polished surfaces with fine grit, and she's had to do the dusting twice.'

Even at this distance . . . The volcano seemed closer to her than Bryn, Tara thought wearily. She could reach out and touch him, but like the orchid encased in its transparent box, the invisible barrier with which he surrounded himself, effectively prevented her from getting close.

The next two days gave her no opportunity to be alone with him, and relief and frustration fought for supremacy as Con and Liz took advantage of the holiday, and accompanied them on each trip out in the jeep. Back at the house, Con annexed Bryn as an automatic right, to talk about the business of the ranch, and the following morning the public holiday was over, and work resumed its normal routine, and it was time for Tara to leave Lamura.

'You're welcome to stay on for as long as you like,' Liz pressed her hospitably at breakfast time.

'I must go—I daren't delay replacing my passport, and I must get in touch with my firm's branch office here,' Tara refused. Every instinct in her cried out to accept Liz's invitation, and remain. Now that the holiday was over, her host and hostess would not be free to go out so much with Bryn, and if she herself went with him each day to visit the colt in the top pasture, who knew, she might eventually manage to penetrate his armour, if not today, then perhaps tomorrow, or the next day . . .

It was wishful thinking. Hopeless wishing. Deep down, she knew it, and the bitterness of it soured her breakfast, so that she crumbled her toast uneaten on her plate, and curled her fingers round her coffee cup for comfort as she insisted with a stubbornness that was akin to desperation,

'I must go. The sooner I deal with the complications of losing the van, the better.' The sooner she could escape from Bryn's orbit, the better, common sense warned her. He dominated her thoughts as well as her actions, and distance might bring him into perspective, she told herself without conviction. It was harder to leave than she had imagined it would be. Con kissed her in a fatherly fashion, and Liz hugged her close and exhorted,

'Come and see us again soon. As soon as you can. You haven't met Anne yet.'

She was not likely to now, Tara thought chokily, but she kept her thoughts to herself and got into the jeep beside Bryn, feeling her eyes sting as she waved back to the two figures waving to her from the verandah.

'Lunch first,' Bryn announced an hour later as he steered the vehicle expertly through the flow of town traffic into a parking lot on the main street.

'I want to go to the Consulate first,' Tara objected. He was doing it again, she realised indignantly. He had scarcely spoken during the journey, and now he was taking control again, dictating what she should do, and when she should do it. Tension erupted into irritability, and she snapped, 'You can eat on your own. We're parting company here,' she declared forthrightly. 'Your responsibility to me is ended. From now on, I'm a free agent.' Free from Bryn. Brave words. Bleak words. The reality of the parting struck her like a physical blow, and unless she left him now, quickly, without a backward look, her defiant façade threatened to crumble like her slice of breakfast toast, and release the brimming tears that made her eyes an angry brilliance as she raised them defiantly to Bryn's face.

'Your appointment with the Consulate isn't until two o'clock,' he told her calmly.

'I haven't made an appointment with the Consulate. I'm just going to drop in on the offchance.'

'Then it's as well I made an appointment for you, otherwise you'd have been politely turned away at the desk, and told to come again tomorrow,' he said evenly.

'You ... did ... *what*?' Tara ground out. His impudence took her breath away. Not so her voice. 'How dare you interfere!' she cried shrilly. From the moment she first set eyes on Bryn he had interfered—with her holiday plans, with her freedom of movement. A mischievous voice inside her added, also with her appetite and her sleep, to say nothing of her heart's peace. She quelled it ruthlessly. 'How dare you?' she demanded furiously.

'I dared because I dislike wasted journeys,' Bryn told her crisply.

'The Consulate's open for business.'

'But exceptionally busy entertaining a large delegation of banana planters,' he interrupted her brusquely. 'They fitted you in at two o'clock as a favour.'

'A favour to whom?' she asked sharply.

'To me,' Bryn answered. 'I happen to be on first-name terms with the Consul.'

A favour to Bryn. Which meant he must have pressed the appointment for her, and that could only mean one thing. He wanted to be rid of her. He wanted to go back to the ranch, and his colt, without being troubled by her unwanted presence. The discovery choked her. She longed to run away and hide, anywhere, so long as she could get away from Bryn before her tears spilled over, and completed her humiliation in front of him. Blindly she spun away from him.

'Tara, hello! Paul said if we came down to the parking lot, you'd just about be coming in.'

'Meli!' Tara stared bewilderedly into her laughing face, at Paul's cheerful grin beside her. 'What a coincidence,' she stammered the first words that came into her head.

'No coincidence,' Paul set her right. 'Bryn phoned to say you'd be coming into town, and it'd be nice if we all had lunch together. So here we are.'

'Bryn phoned?' He had made the arrangements without consulting her, expecting her to fall in with them, because he had made them. Probably expecting her to be grateful, the same as he no doubt thought she should be grateful for the appointment he had fixed for her at the Consulate. Tara threw him a vitriolic look. In his usual high-handed fashion, he had neatly manoeuvred her into a position where she had no option but to accept both the lunch and the appointment, just as he had ensured she accepted his orchid. Seething inwardly, she kept her back carefully turned on Bryn and asked Meli,

'Where's the baby?'

'He's with his doting relatives,' Meli smiled.
'They're making the most of the opportunity, because
Paul and I have just been to finalise the lease of an
apartment. We're moving in next week, and as soon as
we're installed, you'll have to come to the housewarm-
ing. As well as the christening, later on,' she reminded
them gaily.

She said nothing about coming to stay. For a
moment, when Meli mentioned the apartment, Tara's
hopes rose. If she could stay with Meli and Paul, Bryn
would have no possible excuse to detain her any
longer, if her travel documents should take a day or
two to be processed. But reason told her that, with a
new home and a new baby to cope with, Meli would
have her hands full, without wanting the distraction of
a resident guest.

'Since we're to come to you for two parties in a row,
be my guests for lunch today,' Bryn insisted, and
steered them towards a nearby hotel, the name of
which made Tara thankful she had put on a dress. It
was the cream one she had worn for dinner two
evenings before, but without the addition of Bryn's
orchid on the shoulder. Unknown to anyone but
herself, the flower was tucked deep in her borrowed
suitcase among the clothes Liz gave to her. She
scorned her own inability to throw away the orchid.
Twice she made to toss it into the waste paper basket,
and twice she changed her mind. The second time she
thrust it impatiently back into its transparent box, and
hid it out of sight under the clothes in the suitcase,
then slammed the lid shut, deriding her own
cowardice for not making a clean break when she
parted from Bryn, taking nothing with her to remind
her of him. Nothing, except her memories, and the
pain of those must fade with time, or else how could
she continue to exist? she asked herself wretchedly.
She toyed with her food without appetite, and

somehow managed to make the necessary responses to Meli's gay chatter. Fortunately the other couple were full of their own news, of the baby, and their new apartment, and Bryn told them about the colt, and her own lack of enthusiasm went unnoticed in the general criss-cross of talk at the table. Then it was almost two o'clock, and time to leave for her appointment at the Consulate.

'We'll phone you the moment we're in the apartment,' Meli promised as they parted in front of the hotel.

'I don't know where I'll be,' Tara said doubtfully.

'Never mind, we'll ring Bryn,' Paul consoled, taking it for granted she would still remain in touch with Bryn. Just as Bryn took it for granted that he should remain with her during her visit to the Consulate. To Tara's disconcertment, he took his leave of Meli and Paul, and turned to walk with her the hundred yards or so to the Consulate, and was right beside her as she approached the reception desk. She stopped in her tracks at a distance that she hoped was out of earshot of the receptionist, and hissed furiously,

'I can see to this myself, I don't need your supervision!'

'I'll wait for you,' Bryn was unperturbed. 'I know most of the staff here,' he said blandly, 'I'll talk to one of them while you ask about your passport.'

'I don't *want* you to wait. I won't have you riding herd on me,' she countered angrily. She spoke nothing but the truth. She did *not* want Bryn to wait. If he remained by her side for much longer, she told herself desperately, her sorely tried self-control would surely disintegrate, and the tears would spill over, and she would fling herself into his arms and beg him to take her with him, back to Lamura, over to Texas, whenever or wherever he went—she little cared so long as she remained with him. And the shame of his refusal would burn her up and destroy her, like the molten lava had destroyed Mahila. She must not let it happen. Somehow she must get rid of Bryn, and quickly.

'Just *go away*, and leave me alone,' she blurted out, her voice beginning to rise.

'Miss Brodie?'

Tara turned, blinking at the bespectacled member of the Consulate staff, and tried without success to remember why she was here, and what it was she had come about.

'I believe—your passport, Miss Brodie?' he prompted her tactfully, and waited, and Tara clutched urgently at her scattered wits.

'Yes, that's right, my passport,' she remembered thankfully.

'Perhaps you'd like to come over here and sit down, and we'll see what's to be done about it.' To Tara's dismay, the man indicated some comfortable chairs grouped near an occasional table in a corner of the reception area. Was there to be no privacy? She clenched and unclenched her hands nervously. She had envisaged being taken to an office, of going through a door, and leaving Bryn safely on the other side.

'Nice to see you again, Mr Mathieson,' their companion went on amiably. 'Will you be joining the Consul at the reception tonight?' The man's verbal inclusion of Bryn was a tacit invitation to join them, and Tara fumed helplessly as he immediately took advantage of it, and replied easily,

'Not tonight, we'll get together some other time, when David's able to relax. Banana plantations aren't much in my line.'

'No, I imagine not,' their companion laughed, then turned briskly to Tara. 'Now, Miss Brodie, there are one or two questions . . .'

'When shall I get my duplicate documents?' Tara asked anxiously when he had finished.

'Let me see,' the man pursed his lips thoughtfully, 'we shall have to check back with the U.K., of course, that'll take a few days—their Bank Holiday begins at the weekend, as you know.'

'Oh, no!' Tara groaned. 'Not another public holiday! Why couldn't the two coincide? There's part of this week gone already.'

'Exactly. We'll telex straight away, of course, but it may be next week before they're able to give us a reply.'

'A whole week?' Tara breathed her dismay.

'Say about ten days. A fortnight at the most, by the time we've got the documents processed and in your hands.' Her informant spoke as if he was doing her a favour, Tara thought bitterly.

'What am I supposed to do in the meantime?' she questioned him tautly. 'I've got no travel documents, and no money. I suppose I could ask at my firm's branch here for an advance on my salary,' she brightened as the idea occurred to her.

'I understand that Mr Mathieson's taking care of you,' the bespectacled one beamed at her as if he had found a good home for a stray puppy, she thought wrathfully.

'I refuse to impose on Mr Mathieson's generosity any longer.' The cutting edge to her voice was razor sharp, and if it missed the official, it could not fail to reach Bryn. She dared not look at him. Her nerves tingled as she steeled herself for his response.

'It's been my pleasure.' It came, and she could cheerfully have slain him for the laugh in his voice.

'Then I'm sure, for the sake of another ten days or so . . .?' The official looked askance at Bryn.

'Naturally, Miss Brodie's welcome to remain at Lamura until her documents come through.' There was mockery in his tone now, clear and unmistakable, and Tara's eyes snapped as she spun round in her chair to face him.

'That won't be necessary,' she refused flatly. 'Now I'm in town, I intend to remain here, and my firm will find me suitable accommodation until my documents come through,' she stated confidently.

She marched into the travel agency, uncaring this time that Bryn was with her. Let him come if he wanted to, she gave a mental shrug, he would only have to go back again when she had settled matters with the manager. She was fortunate, he had just finished talking to a group of clients, and she annexed him before he disappeared into his office.

'Accommodation? You must be joking!' To her dismay he laughed her request out of court. 'The only rooms left are in the five-star class, and ten days' stay at that level would be way above any advance on salary I'm allowed to offer you. Don't look a gift horse in the mouth,' he told Tara bluntly, 'take Mr Mathieson's offer and stay on at Lamura, and thank your lucky stars you've got a roof over your head.' He ignored Tara's desperate signals for silence and went on cheerfully, 'You know what it's like here, in the middle of the tourist season, there've even been people sleeping out on the beaches this year.'

'I know,' Tara admitted hastily, willing to do anything to sidetrack him, 'but surely you could send me out on one of the long-distance touring coaches, they offer automatic accommodation for the courier.'

'You must know I can't do that,' the man said regretfully. 'I can't use your services at all, until you've had your passport replaced. Be reasonable, Tara,' he begged, and Tara's lips thinned. The last thing she felt like at the moment was being reasonable, particularly with Bryn standing beside her, listening interestedly to every word that was being said. 'The only long-distance coaches going out this week are all on tours to the mainland, and you know it'd be no use trying to explain to the Immigration authorities there that you lost your passport in the tidal wave. They'd simply turn you back at the docks, and leave the coach without a courier. Take a fortnight's paid leave,' he offered generously, 'and treat yourself to an extended holiday. That's the most I can do for you,' he stated finally, 'and I'm sure Mr Mathieson would agree that it's the best solution.'

'Oh, absolutely,' Bryn agreed suavely, and Tara stiffened at the jeering undertone that grated like a rasp on her sensitive pride. Bryn took her by the arm, and her rigid muscles became jelly at the first touch of his fingers, sending an urgent warning, if she still needed one, that she had to get away from him quickly, before the will to do so deserted her. She drew in a long, uneven breath, and cast frantically about her for a solution that would give her her freedom, and dredged up the only plausible one that she could think of.

'I'll go to the car hire firm to settle about the caravanette,' she decided, grasping at straws, 'and ask them to hire me another vehicle for the next fortnight.'

'Ah, yes,' the manager brightened, 'I forgot to mention your caravanette.' He smiled happily, thankful to be able to impart at least one piece of good news. 'The agency uses that particular car hire firm a good deal, on special discount terms. But you know that, of course.' Tara nodded. 'As soon as I heard what had happened to the caravanette, I rang their manager, and it seems you'd taken advantage of the special arrangement we have with them for hirings by members of our own staff, so the vehicle was automatically covered by our own insurance company.' So Bryn would not be held responsible for the van's loss after all. Almost, Tara wished the special terms

did not apply. Steadfastly she refused to look at Bryn,
refused to read the 'I told you so' expression that must
surely be on his face as the manager went on, 'I
contacted the insurers as well, and they're settling for
the loss of the caravanette in full, direct to the car hire
company. It'll take a few weeks, of course, these things
always do.' The familiar refrain, Tara thought
irritably, and nerved herself to listen to what she knew
must come next, 'Until the claim's finally settled you
won't be able to hire another vehicle from them, but as
soon as it's been cleared you'll be able to go ahead and
choose whichever van you want.'

By that time it would be too late. She had fought,
and lost, and Bryn had won, and she was too tired to
fight any longer. Her feet dragged and she felt like a
prisoner in chains as she walked out of the door beside
him. The bright sunshine mocked her as the brightly
dressed holiday crowd carried them along beside lawns
turned to green velvet by copious water showers from
revolving standpipes, and flanked with brilliant flower
beds that at any other time would have drawn Tara's
eyes with delight.

Two weeks. The words hammered on her mind like
a judge's sentence. The last three days had been
almost impossible to live through, but if she could
have left Bryn now, right away, there still might have
been a chance, just the faintest chance, that she could
salvage enough of her battered heart to keep it beating
through the bleak years ahead. Now it was too late. At
the end of another fortnight, of seeing Bryn every day,
being with him, talking to him, when the time came
for her to leave Lamura for good, she knew
despairingly that her heart would for ever, irrevocably,
remain behind with him.

Cool spray touched her bare arm, wetly caressing,
and Bryn guided her round the damp area of the paving
where the wind blew the spray from the water

showers, slipping his hand down from her elbow to her waist to draw her away from the wetness. The movement brought her closer to him, close enough to feel the lithe movement of his flat-hipped stride against her, carefully checked to keep pace with her much shorter step. The crowds thinned, making walking easier, but still he held her against him, and Tara felt weakly incapable of pulling herself free. A curious lethargy crept over her, subduing the fiery spirit that burned inside her like the fire in the heart of the orchid, and she made no resistance when Bryn turned her away from the thoroughfare on to the beach, and walked along, parallel with the water.

Surfboarders rode the combers, that showed no signs of their recent turbulence. The fury of the storm was over, for the islands. For herself, it had only just begun. The warm breeze fanned her cheeks, bringing with it the shouts and laughter of the surfboarders, and rustling a canopy of palm fronds above them. The faint, familiar sound stung her into an awareness of her surroundings, and she glanced upwards uneasily, recollection of the dent left on the van bonnet by the shattered coconut, still vivid in her mind.

'Scared?'

Bryn's taunt swung her eyes back to meet his, and a flash of her old spirit sparked their gold flecks into life again.

'No, I was just hoping,' she retorted swiftly, an upsurge of temper reviving her flagging will. She might have lost the battle, but at least she would go down fighting, she rallied herself. Bryn should not be allowed to have things all his own way, even now. 'I was just hoping that, if a coconut did come down, it might land on your head, as you richly deserve,' she declared vindictively.

'You little spitfire!' he ejaculated, and there was a bright glint in his eyes as he swung her round to face him. 'I can see it's going to take longer to tame you than I bargained for!'

'You've only got a couple of weeks to try,' she flung back at him recklessly. 'If it's going to take twice that long to gentle your colt, what chance do you think you stand with me?' If he kissed her, it would not take two minutes, let alone two weeks, she told herself despairingly, but Bryn must not be allowed to guess that, and she rushed on blindly, using words to armour herself against him. 'You might just as well give up now and let me go, a fortnight's not long enough,' she goaded him.

'Then it's best not to waste any time,' he gritted, and pressed his lips hungrily down upon her mouth. It was useless to struggle. His arms held her in a vice, his lips held her in thrall, and with a tiny, inarticulate moan of submission, Tara knew she was lost. He felt her yield against him, and immediately his kiss changed, and deepened, its demand became a seeking, its pressure, a gentle caress. His lips left her mouth and began to wander, exploring along the delicate line of her jaw, and finally came to rest in the warm, throbbing hollow of her throat.

'Tara, Tara,' he groaned, 'I can't let you go.' She quivered under his touch and went deathly still, and he raised a tormented face to hers. 'I can't imagine life without you. Don't leave me. Don't go,' he begged her brokenly.

'Bryn, I . . .' she began haltingly, and he stopped her words with urgent kisses.

'Don't say it. Don't say you'll leave me. Please, give me a chance,' he begged. 'I love you, Tara . . . my heart . . . my darling . . .' His lips punctuated his vow, pressing against her own with a desperate entreaty. 'I love you.'

'I can't leave you until I get my passport.' Tara's weakness suddenly became her strength, and words rushed from her.

'Your passport? That was only a ploy, to keep you with me. How else could I make you come to Lamura, instead of going to stay with Meli and Paul?'

How else? How could he ask? Tara stared at him in stunned amazement.

'Oh, the lies I told you, to keep you with me,' Bryn confessed. 'I couldn't bear to lose you. I can't bear it now.' The prospect unmanned him, and he buried his agony in the softness of her hair.

'Bryn, don't.' Tara reached up and drew his face down to her own, gently smoothing her fingers along the pale lines that fanned out from the corners of his eyes, tiny smile lines, that now felt suspiciously damp beneath her fingertips. 'How can I leave you, when I love you?' she whispered.

Only the wind in the palm fronds knew how long it took her to convince him of her love, endless, tender minutes of rapture, safe in the circle of Bryn's arms, as he murmured soft answers to questions she no longer needed to ask, while his lips caressed her own, and time stood still.

At last she stirred, and the single shadow on the sand became recognisably two shadows again, though still closely linked, with Bryn's arm round her waist, holding her tightly as if even now he was afraid to let her go.

'Will we ever go back to Mahila, do you think?' They stopped at the water's edge and gazed out across the combers to the distant spiral of smoke still lazily rising on the far horizon.

'One day, when it's safe again,' Bryn promised, and smiled down at her, the deep, contented smile of a man who holds all of his world in his arms, 'and in the meantime there'll always be a part of us there, beside the tide pool, watching the rainbows on the bluff. That reminds me,' he fumbled in his pocket, 'I brought a souvenir away from the island for you.'

'A souvenir? Not a piece of lava rock?' she teased.

'Something much nicer. Let me see if it fits.' He took the third finger of her left hand between his own and gently slid something along it. 'It's a perfect fit,' he discovered with satisfaction.

'It's beautiful!' Wonderingly Tara turned the ring of rose-pink coral round and round on her finger, exclaiming at the intricately carved design.

'The pink coral's found at great depth,' Bryn told her, watching her pleasure with pleased eyes. 'It's very slow growing, which makes it fairly rare, and very precious.' His eyes said the wearer was more rare and precious to him than all the pink coral in the Pacific, and he trailed tender lips across Tara's cheeks, that warmed to match her ring as she read the message in his eyes.

'I had it made specially for you,' he enhanced her pleasure in his gift. 'One of the fishermen on Mahila carves coral to augment his income, and he had this pink piece, so I asked him to guess your size, and make the ring for you. It was the day we watched the rainbows together,' he remembered happily.

'You didn't tell me.' If only he had told her then, how many dark hours might have been prevented, but it did not matter now. The dark hours were behind her, as were their shadows on the sand.

'I wasn't sure you'd accept it,' he confessed humbly. 'So I kept it, hoping against hope, and now,' his smile proclaimed the wait worth while, 'it'll do until we can choose a proper engagement ring together.'

'Let this be my engagement ring?' Tara begged eagerly. 'No diamonds can possibly compare with this, for me. The coral ring's special, because you had it made for me, because it came from Mahila where we met.' The glow in his eyes told her her words had pleased him, that the rose pink ring was special to him, too, for the same reason.

'In that case, I'll buy you an eternity ring to go with it,' he capitulated, 'so long as you wear your coral ring to let the world know you're mine.' He folded her back hungrily into his arms. 'There's plenty of time to get the eternity ring,' he murmured in her ear.

'You've only got a fortnight,' she teased him wickedly.

'A fortnight's just right to complete the formalities,' he answered swiftly, 'and then. . . .' he paused.

'And then?' she prompted him, suddenly shy.

'We'll spend our honeymoon somewhere where I don't have to share you with other people,' he declared possessively.

'It won't be safe to go back to Mahila yet,' she demurred.

'I wasn't thinking of Mahila,' he shook his head. 'That island was much too heavily populated for my liking,' he exaggerated ruefully, 'I scarcely had you to myself for more than five minutes at a time.'

'Where, then?' She did not care where, so long as they were together.

'The *Gull* will be ready to put to sea by the time we're ready.' The ardent fire in his eyes told her it could not be soon enough for him, and he cupped her flushed cheeks in his two hands and pressed them against his own as he went on, 'on the *Gull* we can go where we like, do what we please, and be completely alone,' he anticipated contentedly. 'We'll do something different, if you'd rather?' His eager gaze begged her not to change his plan.

'There's nothing I'd like better,' she assured him happily. 'I'm longing to see the *Gull*. Is she anything like the *Roseanne*?'

'Better,' he boasted promptly, 'though I'm thinking of re-naming her.' He waited, his look teasing her.

'Re-naming her? What?' she looked up expectantly.

'I thought of calling her *Mahila*,' he suggested.

'That way, we'll always keep a part of the island with us, wherever we go.'

'I thought you might re-name her after your wife,' she suggested demurely, and Bryn looked at her doubtfully, but her dancing eyes betrayed her, and his brow cleared.

'I couldn't call her after you.' His lips pressed his explanation onto her own, with long pauses in between to add emphasis to his words.

'There can only . . ever . . . be one Tara . . . for me,' he told her huskily.

ROMANCE

Variety is the spice of romance

Each month, Mills and Boon publish new romances. New stories about people falling in love. A world of variety in romance — from the best writers in the romantic world. Choose from these titles in May.

THE STREET OF THE FOUNTAIN Madeleine Ker
RUTHLESS IN ALL Jessica Steele
BY LOVE BEWITCHED Violet Winspear
MOONDRIFT Anne Mather
THE INWARD STORM Penny Jordan
TAKE HOLD OF TOMORROW Daphne Clair
SPANISH SERENADE Mary Lyons
EVERLASTING LOVE Carole Mortimer
DEVIL WITHIN Catherine George
SAVAGE SUMMER Sue Peters
DANCE WHILE YOU CAN Claire Harrison
PRINCESS Alison Fraser

On sale where you buy paperbacks. If you require further information or have any difficulty obtaining them, write to: Mills & Boon Reader Service, PO Box 236, Thornton Road, Croydon, Surrey CR9 3RU, England.

Mills & Boon

the rose of romance

4 BOOKS FREE

Enjoy a Wonderful World of Romance...

M/4
SP6M

Passionate and intriguing, sensual and exciting. A top quality selection of four Mills & Boon titles written by leading authors of Romantic fiction can be delivered direct to your door absolutely FREE!

Try these Four Free books as your introduction to Mills & Boon Reader Service. You can be among the thousands of women who enjoy six brand new Romances every month PLUS a whole range of special benefits.

- Personal membership card.
- Free monthly newsletter packed with recipes, competitions, exclusive book offers and a monthly guide to the stars.
- Plus extra bargain offers and big cash savings.

There is no commitment whatsoever, no hidden extra charges and your first parcel of four books is absolutely FREE!

Why not send for more details now? Simply complete and send the coupon to MILLS & BOON READER SERVICE, P.O. BOX 236, THORNTON ROAD, CROYDON, SURREY, CR9 3RU, ENGLAND. OR why not telephone us on 01-684 2141 and we will send you details about the Mills & Boon Reader Service Subscription Scheme – you'll soon be able to join us in a wonderful world of Romance.

Please note:– READERS IN SOUTH AFRICA write to
Mills & Boon Ltd., Postbag X3010, Randburg 2125, S. Africa.

Please send me details of the Mills & Boon Reader Service Subscription Scheme.

NAME (Mrs/Miss) _____ EP6

ADDRESS _____

_____

COUNTY/COUNTRY _____

POSTCODE _____

BLOCK LETTERS PLEASE